ARE YOU READY...

THE LIE

KYM STREAT

Ark House Press
PO Box 1722, Port Orchard, WA 98366 USA
PO Box 1321, Mona Vale NSW 1660 Australia
PO Box 318 334, West Harbour, Auckland 0661 New Zealand
arkhousepress.com

Cataloguing in Publication Data:
Title: The Lie
ISBN: 978-0-6480508-7-2 (pbk.)
Subjects: Fiction
Other Authors/Contributors: Streat, Kym

Design and layout by initiateagency.com

To Andrew, my biggest fan, husband and friend.
Thank you for continually encouraging me.

To my Lord Jesus... whom I owe everything!

To all those who are seeking for God's truth...

Dear Reader,

This has taken years, so long in fact that I nearly gave up. If it weren't for God and my husband's promptings, then this would have stayed dormant on my hard drive forever. However, the niggling and nagging to finish this kept gnawing at my heart; maybe because it's truth or maybe it's simply hoping that someone will gain inspiration to pick up the Bible and research the subject for themselves.

Ultimately… you'll be the judge, but whatever you decide, decide to be strong in God for the times ahead.

Kym

C H A P T E R O N E

Year 1831

Tommy awoke from his deep sleep. Startled by the bell ringing, his faced grimaced as he squinted at his watch. It read 1.15 am. *What does Father Harvey want at this hour?* he wondered. He quickly got to his feet, put on his trousers and boots and rushed next door to Father Harvey's room, and softly knocked on his door.

Father Harvey opened the door abruptly and said, "Tommy my boy, I'm sorry to wake you at this hour, but I need you to prepare the horses."

"Is everything all right Father?"

"No, I must get back to Evensmore tonight!"

"But Father, that's over five hours in travel, we've just arrived today and the horses are already spent…and what about your brother's funeral tomorrow?"

"Tommy, please just do as I say!" Father Harvey said flustered, as he turned and closed the door behind him.

Charger stood a menacing 19 hands high and Dom was just a tad under. Their massive heads hung over their stall doors while they rested, the breath from their nostrils condensed and furled upward in the autumn chill. Charger, the bigger and eldest of the two horses, was the first to notice the lantern coming toward the stables, he let out a soft whinny at seeing his friend entering.

Tommy rushed towards their stalls, grabbing their lead ropes on the way. He took Charger's head with both hands and looked him square in the eyes. "Now Charger, I need all you've got, Father needs us tonight." He moved over to Dom who was now wide-awake and vying for Tommy's attention. "Dom," he said, "you do everything Charger does okay boy, no folly tonight my friend. We have important business to attend to."

Father Harvey was busily writing down the dream he'd been given. Carefully noting every detail, it was so clear in his head but his shaking hand was making it near impossible for his words to be legible. His emotions overtook him. "Oh Lord, forgive me...I must stop Father Daniel before he delivers this message." he cried out.

Emily Tucker was fast asleep. "Emmmiilyyy...Emmmiiilyyy my darling...wake up my child." The soothing, melting voice slowly drew sixteen-year-old Emily out of her deep dreamy sleep. She looked, and hovering above her was Crystalyn, her spirit friend, with his glow radiating the room and his rather sickly sweet smile warming her face. *He was so handsome,* she thought, his golden locks falling gently across his boyish features. She admired his little pixie like face and his tiny transparent wings that seemed to drum a 100 beats a second. She loved Crystalyn, he had become her best friend, someone who she could confide in and trust with her life. "Crystalyn my friend," she called and happily grinned as she stretched, "what are you doing at this hour, why did you have to wake me. Is something wrong?"

"Emily, dear Emily, I must get you to deliver a message to the Chief, sweet girl," his liquid honey voice crooned, making her heart melt.

"At this hour?" She smiled and giggled. "I can't Crystalyn, it'll have to wait until the morning!" she said wearily. "I'm tired and it's too cold to go out. Besides, what's the urgency?"

"Emily, it is very, very important. You must get up and go now," he insisted trying to sound soft and gentle but with a coldness coming through.

Emily yawned and stretched again as she rolled over burying her face back into her pillow and mumbled, "No Crystalyn, I can't, its 2.15... I'll do it later this morning."

"Emily please," he crooned and stroked her cheek.

"No, I'm just too tired; I'll do it in the morning."

"Emily!" Crystalyn raised his voice sternly. "You'll Go Now. Now I say!"

Crystalyn watched as Emily crept quietly out the door, so not to wake her siblings, and headed off down the foggy lane way.

"You're getting less tactful you know Crystalyn, she'll start to see through your charm."

Crystalyn whipped around to face the voice in the darkness. "What would you know Crechus?" he spat and hissed. The glow emanating around his handsome pixie like figure quickly vanishing, revealing a black hideous being with mottled sinewy skin, red eyes, and dark vascular bat wings. "She's just an expendable pawn in the grand plan, there's plenty more where she came from," Crystalyn stated.

"Maybe... but you'd better hope you're right, else Master will have you fried," Crechus said as he burst out laughing. His bulging eyes closed as his sharp taloned hands covered his grotesque facial features in amusement, his black wings and body shook with his rumbling chuckles.

"Shut up you idiot," Crystalyn snapped.

Emily trudged through the streets, holding her coat tight around her to keep the biting cold out. *What is it with Crystalyn lately?* she mused. *He used to be fun but now, he's getting too serious and pushy. I'll have to tell him that I do not like his attitude lately.*

John Barnes, Chief of Evensmore Police, heard a soft knock at his door downstairs. His wife awoke. "What is it?" she whispered.

"Go back to sleep. It's nothing," said John.

He lit the lantern and quickly descended the stairs and opened the door to find Emily shaking with cold. "What are you doing here?" he snapped angrily.

"Crystalyn told me to come and give you a message."

He leaned out the door. "Did anyone see you?" he questioned, whilst his eyes scanned the surrounds.

"No, well I don't think so, surely not at this hour anyway."

Charger and Dom were at full speed, their massive hooves pounding and shaking the stony ground beneath them. The carriage was loudly rattling and shaking as it careered through the forest road. Father Harvey was busily trying to piece together everything he'd seen and heard in his dream. He was fervently praying that Father Daniel would receive his message with an open heart and he could stop what they had both started.

Angelic Captains Chale and Jophiel were gripping the sides of the carriage towards the front. Lieutenants Seth and Gabe were toward the back, their large majestic angelic wings flat on their backs so not to create any wind drag for the horses, their glory dulled to keep them unnoticed by the enemy. Their focus was ahead, watching intently for any signs that the enemy had gotten word of their mission. It was imperative that their Lord's message got to its destination without fail.

David Carter's house was in silence, in the still of the night everyone was peacefully sleeping in his household. He stirred as he heard a faint tapping at his bedroom window. He looked out toward the noise and his heart sank. He quietly got up, went down the hallway, and opened his front door.

"I've come to call in that favour," John Barnes demanded. David let out a deep sigh and hung his head low. "Remember... you've taken the oath," John smirked.

David closed the door, went to the cloakroom, put on his overcoat, and stepped out into the frigid night air.

Tommy was focused, Charger and Dom were sound horses, and he had faith that they would get them back home safely, but still he diligently watched the road like a hawk. *The moon was bright lighting the way clearly but the shadows where eerie tonight.* Tommy thought. He wished he was back in his bunk asleep and this was all just a bad dream.

The horses' hooves made the loud rumbling, pounding sound down the road, the carriage rattled and creaked, waxing and waning at every corner and bump along the road. The thin wooden wheels were biting into the gravel, grappling the road for grip.

"Are you alright Father?" Tommy yelled back, worried that the old carriage wouldn't hold up to the careering speed.

"Yes Tommy, keep going." Father hung his head out the window and urged Tommy onward.

Tommy hung tightly onto the leather reins; they were straining and stretching under the force of the horses against them. His hands started blistering and bleeding from steering the massive team at such a speed.

Then suddenly, there was a deafening crack echoing throughout the moist night air… and then… there was nothing.

A dark ominous being stood waiting in the bushes "We've got them." he shouted. They won't get through with this message. Are you ready to fight?" he asked the other demons gathered with him.

"Always," they shouted in unison before they pushed forward in their rage for battle.

Silence hit Tommy, like a thick heavy blanket, it filled the night as blackness crept over him. The moonlight glistened on the sweat of the horses' coats. The smell of dirt, sweat, and death lingered in the air. Hours slipped by.

David Carter removed his heavy damp overcoat and mud caked boots, he quietly slipped back into his bed.

It's so quiet! Tommy thought, *what's going on?* Tommy awoke with the gritty taste of gravel mixed with blood and saliva in his mouth. "What's happened?" he whispered, confused and dazed. "How long have I been here? Aaaaaaaagggghh." His cry ripped and echoed through the silent night. He looked down at the gash in his right side and the obscure lump jutting out. *A broken rib*, he thought. "Aaaaahhhhhh... Noooo." He buckled under the excruciating pain emanating from his right leg. He looked down and gazed upon its crookedness. He felt blood slowly seeping down his forehead.

Where am I? What am I doing on the road? He thought franticly, his mind reeling trying to piece together the recent events, but only returning blank. He slowly manoeuvred his body into a position where he could look around. The road ahead to Evensmore was clear. "Where is everyone?" he whispered. He slowly turned, carefully to not cause himself more pain and checked the road behind him. His face recoiled in agony with images that burned into his conscience forever.

He gently rolled onto his left side and slowly dragged himself back towards the horses; sobs rose up into his throat like knots, like lumps fighting to get out all at once.

He reached Dom first. Tommy's body convulsed and the heavy sobs poured out as he looked upon Dom's twisted neck and crumpled frame lying entangled in the leather harness. Tommy reached out his hand to touch his friend; his body was motionless and cold from the night, his coat still sticky from the sweat mixed with heavy dew, his eyes were pale, dull, and lifeless.

He looked up ahead and saw Charger lying behind and off to one side of Dom's body. He slid towards him and then laid his hand upon the big horse's neck. "Oh Charger," he cried. Hot tears started to flow down his face, stinging the grazes and gravelled gouges etched into his raw cheeks.

He lifted his hand and saw Charger's thick sticky blood caked to it, glistening black under the moonlight. *Maybe one of the horses stumbled. Or... or there was a hole that we didn't see...why can't I remember?* he wondered as he continued to sob and try and work out what had happened, but unable to recall anything. Confused he reached out to run his hand down Charger's forehead and felt the syrupy congealing liquid slowly leaching out. "What happened?" Tommy whispered as he quickly slid himself around to get a better look at Charger's face.

He looked closely and wiped away the blood from Charger's forehead to reveal a large jagged cavernous hole with bone fragments clinging to the clotted blood.

He recognised it instantly. "A gunshot wound!" He exclaimed and reeled back frantically looking around for a stranger in the night. "Who would do such a thing? Oh no, Father," he whispered in bewilderment and horror. "Father," he shouted frantically, "Father Harvey can you hear me? Are you all right?"

Tommy desperately dragged himself to the carriage that lay broken on its side, wincing at every move, he looked inside, and it was empty. Distressed, he called out again, "Father Harvey." Nothing! He slid himself toward the back of the carriage and saw a still figure lying

8

twisted and bloodied on the road. There was no life here.

Tommy started to weep, the pain was too much, confusion and silence overcame him, the night closed in and the darkness swept him away.

Chale, Jophiel, Seth, and Gabe stood before Darius, the Major General of the Lord's angelic regiment. Darius looked upon their battered and bruised bodies, torn wings and defeated, despondent faces. "What happened Chale?" Darius asked sympathetically.

"We were ambushed sir, attacked from behind, they were everywhere. They knew! Five attacked me when I looked up and saw the lone figure standing in the middle of the roadway. But it was too late, the big horse went down."

"What of the Saint?"

"I'm sorry sir!" Chale looked down with tears in his eyes.

"And the boy?"

"He survives," Chale replied.

"Then it has begun."

Present Day

"Daddy, can I get a pony?"

Jack Daley looked down into his 10-year-old daughter's clear, innocent blue eyes and his heart melted. He looked back at Jenny his wife, she smiled and gave him that knowing look of, *you knew this was coming eventually.*

"Well if Sarah gets a pony, I'm getting a motorbike dad," his 12-year-old son Matthew stated.

"Well let's just talk about this later; right now, we're here to listen to God's word." He smiled down at both of them as they climbed the stairs to the old church building.

"Good morning Jack, great to see you here today." Pastor Peter McKinley grabbed Jack's hand shaking it fervently. "Jenny, Matthew, oh, and little Sarah...welcome!"

"How are you Pastor McKinley?" Jack replied.

"Very well, very well indeed, it's such a beautiful day isn't it? And please Jack, thank you for the respect, but just call me Peter."

"Yes, certainly Peter," Jack said as they shuffled through the door to find their seats.

It was a small church of about one hundred people. This was a vast difference from the city church of 7000 members from where Jack and his family had previously attended. With church interest's groups, over forties, fifties and sixties, you name it they had it. *Yep*, he thought, *this is the place to be, one service that finished whenever God said it could.* It was nothing for the worship to continue for hours sometimes until 2 pm. *The Spirit of God really moves here*, Jack thought to himself, *I didn't realize how much I needed this place.*

He looked over at Jenny sitting beside him, *how beautiful she was*, he thought. "Thank you, God, for my gorgeous wife," he whispered. She heard him, smiled, and squeezed his arm. The service was about to start.

On the roof sat Chale and Jophiel, along with a hundred of the Lord's angels scattered around the old church grounds. Chale looked at Jophiel and smiled, his features chiselled, his blonde hair gently shifted in the breeze. They had been friends for eons and had proudly fought many battles together.

Jophiel was the opposite of Chale in many ways, dark hair, olive completion, but both were strong and mighty in their stature. No demon could out manoeuvre these two Captains. "I know Chale," Jophiel said grinning at him, "this is your favourite day!" he laughed, but still kept vigilant.

Chale laid down relaxing his back on the warmth of the iron roof, his mighty sword by his side; he closed his eyes and took in the music and singing that was emanating from the building beneath. "I love you my Lord Jesus," he whispered, listening as other angels joined in the praises. Like ribbons of colourful hues, the songs flowed upward into the heavens praising their King.

"They don't realise how important their praises are for us," Jophiel commented. "Battles have been won and lost on the account of worshipping and praying saints."

"But today ALL is well," Chale replied as he smiled and stretched out his wings, basking in the morning sunrays.

Jophiel laughed at his friend as he stood to survey the surrounding grounds, "Yes, all is well today."

"Do I have to go to school today?" Matthew whined to his mother.

"Yes, you do!" shouted his sister Sarah at the top of her lungs from her bedroom.

Matthew rolled his eyes towards his sister's room. Jenny smiled and gave him a hug. "Come on, otherwise you'll be late," she said.

The three of them walked down the driveway to the front gate and waited for the school bus to arrive. "I'm glad we moved here mummy," Sarah said.

"Me too," Jenny smiled.

"I really thought I wouldn't like it because I'd miss my friends, but now I have lots of new friends." Sarah grinned.

"What about you Matthew? Do you like our new home?" Jenny asked.

"Yeah, it's okay I guess, but I still miss home," he replied.

Matthew had found it harder to adapt to the new school, and making new friends seemed more difficult for him. Sarah however took to it like a duck to water. They all looked up to see the old yellow school bus rattling down the gravel road.

"You have fun today," Jenny said.

"Bye mum," Matthew and Sarah both chorused as they boarded the bus.

Jenny meandered back down the driveway towards the house; she was content here. However, having her parents so far away was hard. She missed them but knew that this was the best decision they had made for a long time; they had to get out of the city. Jack was stressed, and there wasn't any family time any more. *I'm so thankful that Jack gave it up* she thought and smiled briefly pondering over how Jack had always stood out; he was handsome, strong, and stylish. He'd had so much success in his career, but was willing to move for them, and escape the rat race. Their life had become just too fast, b*ut not here in Evensmore,* she thought, *this place is like a time unto itself.*

Jack was sitting in his office downstairs typing an email and attaching the software requirements' document to send to head office. The software company Jack worked for had begged him not to leave, he was a highly skilled, first-rate engineer and they didn't want to lose him. However, Jack knew that he had to put his family first, not his career that had taken precedent for so long. Therefore, they compromised, as long as they could keep him Jack could work from anywhere he chose. There were still the occasional meetings that he physically needed to attend but they would pay all his travel expenses and besides, he actually seemed to get more done now. There were no office politics or people sticking their heads in for a chat. Jack thought, *I now have the perfect world.* He thoroughly loved his work and was excited about the project he was working on. He was so proud that he had created the new technology and couldn't wait to get it to the world. He hit 'Send' on the email.

"You want a coffee?" Jenny called out.

"Sure do!" Jack replied as he slowly got up out of his chair, stretched and walked up the stairs into the kitchen. "And a cookie?" he questioned hopefully.

Jenny smiled at him. "How are you going with the project?" Jenny asked as she handed him the coffee and biscuit.

"Good so far, no hitches that I can see."

"Great, more time for us." She sidled up to him and gave him a hug. "I love you so much and I'm very proud of you."

"And why would that be?" he smiled down at her.

"Well, you know, this was a big change for you, leaving your fancy office, and moving out here to the country."

"Well it's worked out okay, I'm pretty much my own boss now and this place is great - I get to have coffee with my stunning wife whenever I want to, who could ask for more!" He squeezed Jenny tightly.

"So, what are your thoughts on the pony?" Jenny asked.

"Well, she has wanted one for so long, and I guess there is no real reason why she can't have one now that we have a few acres."

Jenny beamed as she said so excitedly, "Oh she is going to be so thrilled I can't wait to see her face when we tell her."

"Me too and Matthew when we tell him he can finally have that motor bike."

Lora March ran upstairs in tears to her bedroom.

"Come here young lady," the voice of Reverend Jim March bellowed. "I will not tolerate your attitude in my house."

"Leave me alone," the 14-year-old, cried out, "You don't understand, you NEVER understand!"

"Lora, you will not go to that party, it is not the image that we Marchs' want to portray, do you hear me?"

Lora buried her face in her pillow and screamed, her hot tears soaking into the soft down, her face red and angry. "I hate him, I hate him, I hate him!" she exploded concealing her cries into the soft feathers.

The demon named Rebellion stood over her, busily whispering, "He thinks he is so righteous, and who does he think he is? He can't rule your life, you're an adult now, you can do what you want and you don't have to do what he says anymore." Lora was taking in all that Rebellion was saying to her.

Reverend Jim March was angry, very angry. *How dare she disrespect my authority! Doesn't she understand their position in the community, the image that they need to uphold? I am a man of God; a member of the clergy and my family must remain in good standing with the community. I can't have my daughter showing disobedience, she must submit to my authority.* His thoughts ran wild. Once again Rebellion rubbed his hands with delight, he certainly was stirring up trouble in this household and he loved it.

Two little hideous, scaly demonic imps named Pride and Control, were also jumping up and down with glee, shouting thoughts into Jim's mind, coaxing him into an angry stupor. "Yeah, yeah, keep going Pride, that's a good one," said Control grinning with excitement at the discord that they had just created this afternoon in the household.

"Well you need to see ol man Jackson!" Ned Tucker, the local grocer exclaimed. "He deals in horses around here, I'm sure he'll have just the one for yer little girl."

"So where is exactly, Mr Jackson's place?" Jack asked as he handed over his card to pay for the groceries he just purchased.

"He's just up the road a bit from ya's, not far at all. He's got the big old sign over the gate that says, 'Jackson's Farm', can't miss it even if ya tried!"

"Okay great, thanks Mr Tucker."

"Oh, just call me Ned, you city folk are just too formal," he chuckled and smiled.

"Okay, thanks Ned, I'll see you later," Jack replied as he walked out onto the front porch of the store smack into Bill Johnson.

"Hey Jack, are you coming to the men's group tonight?" Bill asked.

"Hi Bill, sorry, I didn't mean to bump into you, Yes I'll be there, looking forward to it actually."

"Great to have you folks in town, I'll see you tonight!"

"Yep see you then," Jack said as he walked over to his car, sat down and took a moment and prayed, "Lord, thank you so much for this wonderful town, bless the people of Evensmore for their kindness and acceptance of my family."

Sixty feet away stood two scaly black demons, one much larger than the other listening to Jack's prayers. "Here's another saint praying," the smaller exclaimed in a whiny voice, his fangs like fine needles showing as he sneered.

"Hmm...We'll have to fix that, we don't need any more of them here," said the larger demon.

Jack drove off unbeknownst to him with his two guardian angels; Lieutenants Gabe and Seth had been assigned to him and were sitting on top of his vehicle. They made eye contact with the two demons as the vehicle sped away.

"They think they're sooooooo good," the smaller demon wiggled his sinewy body in mockery.

"Not for long," the larger one replied sinisterly. "Soon they will be feeling the blades of our swords and face their defeat."

"Yeah, yeah, yeah, take that you fools." The smaller one jumped around waving his sword in the air acting out a mock battle.

Suddenly the larger demon grabbed the smaller one by his spindly arm and jerked him around, his piercing red eyes boring into him, his large talons digging into his slimy, pungent flesh. Bearing his large canine fangs, he growled in contempt of the little imp in his grasp whilst he spat, "Don't take this lightly you idiot; we must keep the saints prayers to a minimum. Stop acting like an imbecile and get to work." And with a hard smack, the small demon landed 30 feet down the road.

CHAPTER THREE

Jack pulled up at the entry of Jackson's farm. He turned and entered the long dirt driveway up to the old farmhouse. It was a neat, white wooden house with the veranda all the way around the front and a quaint little flower garden running along the bottom. *Someone has a green thumb* Jack thought.

Jack got out of his car, walked up the stairs and knocked on the door. He stood waiting as he heard some clattering of dishes then footsteps coming towards the doorway.

The door opened and an elderly man dressed in dark blue overalls stood there smiling. "Good afternoon, what can I do for ya?" he welcomed smiling.

"Ah…Hello Mr Jackson? My name is Jack Daley," Jack said as he held out his hand and shook the man's hand. "Ned Tucker, from the grocery store said that you sell horses and I'm looking for a quiet pony for my daughter Sarah."

"Oh well, you've come to the right place, come in, would ya like a coffee?"

"Yes, that would be great!"

Over the cup of coffee Jack told Ben Jackson about his family, why they moved, how much they loved their new life and the people here at

Evensmore, and Mr Jackson happily listened enjoying the company.

"So how long have you been selling horses?" asked Jack.

"All my life, it's in my blood. My daddy, granddaddy, and great granddaddy bought, sold, and trained horses. Back then it was mainly work horses for pull'en carts and ploughs, now-a-days folks just buy them for pleasure or fancy riding." Mr Jackson pointed to a photo on the wall. "That's my great granddad there when he was just sixteen."

Jack got up, walked over to the wall and looked at the old faded black and white photo sitting in the frame. "Wow, they are big horses," he exclaimed.

"Yep, one of the biggest, 19 hands one of them stood. My granddad told me that his father drove the carriage for the local preacher and these were his horses, he used to talk about them all the time he said. Pretty fine animals eh!"

"Yeah, they certainly are." Jack stared intently at the old photo of the boy standing in front of the carriage and horses. "Well, I don't need one *that* big for Sarah," Jack proclaimed as he smiled.

Mr Jackson laughed. "No siree, I've got just the one for your Sarah."

Jack beamed back a smile. "Great! I'll bring my family over on Saturday if that's okay with you."

"That'll be fine."

Saturday came around very quickly, and Jack and Jenny planned to surprise their children first thing.

"No WAY, are you kidding me?" Matthew beamed.

"Oh, WOW a pony!" Sarah squealed in delight.

Jack and Jenny stood watching their children as both of them were jumping up and down and dancing around repeatedly singing tunes about ponies and motorbikes.

"Yes, well this does mean that you both have to do your chores, homework and clean up after yourselves, no more slacking off," Jenny said loudly over their singing.

Matthew and Sarah both nodded enthusiastically and ran out to the car yelling back, "Come on let's go."

No sooner had Jack stopped the car out the front of the Jackson farmhouse, when Sarah burst out running up to the front door and knocked on it. The door opened and a short, attractive, bright-eyed elderly woman looked down at her. "Well you must be Sarah?" she said smiling.

"You must be Mrs Jackson," Sarah replied with a beaming grin.

Jack, Jenny and Matthew proceeded to get out of the car as May Jackson descended the porch stairs with Sarah; she greeted them with a wave. "Hello, welcome!" she said. "I'm May," she explained smiling warmly as she walked over towards them.

"Hello, pleased to meet you," Jack replied, this is Jenny my wife, Matthew my son and I see that you've already met Sarah."

"Yes," she giggled, "she's a sweetie, isn't she?"

"Ah Jack!" Ben Jackson called out as he walked out from the barn, "I thought I could hear May chatting." He smiled.

"Hi Mr Jackson." Jack went through the introductions once again.

"Oh please, call me Ben," he replied. "Well, hello Sarah," he said looking down at her. "You ready to meet your new friend?"

"Yes!" she beamed unable to stand still.

"All right then, walk over this way."

They all followed Ben past the barn toward a wooden fence and looked across a lush grassy field. Ben walked through the paddock gate and let out a loud whistle and they watched as fifteen horses of all colours, shapes and sizes came enthusiastically galloping across the flat toward them and then stopping just before the fence in front of them. The last to arrive was a little 12-hand buckskin pony with a white star on his forehead.

Ben pointed to the buckskin pony and said, "That's him there, that's Mustard."

Mustard pushed through between the other horses that were jostling for attention and stuck his nose through the railing at Sarah.

Sarah put her hand on his muzzle and rubbed it. "Oh, he is so cute," she said with a giggle.

"Yep he's a little beauty," Ben said as he slipped the rope halter over Mustard's head. "Come on little fella," he said as he walked him back through the gate and tied him to the hitching rail out the front of the barn. "I've had him for about a year now. His owner out grew him so I traded him for a bigger horse for her. He's extremely quiet, just right for a beginner, wouldn't hurt a fly."

"He sounds perfect," Jenny said smiling at Jack.

"You folks want a morning snack?" Ben asked. "May makes the finest cakes around."

"Sounds good to me," replied Jack.

"Well that's settled then," Ben said. "Sarah, if you want you can stay out here and get to know your new friend. There's a brush and comb over there if you want to groom him."

"Okay," she replied.

"Me too," said Matthew.

Jack, Jenny, and Ben walked back into the farmhouse. May had already set the table. They sat down and May poured the tea and handed each of them a slice of her freshly baked orange and poppy seed cake.

"Oh May, this is delicious," Jenny exclaimed.

"She's the best cook in Evensmore," Ben replied as he looked at May and rubbed her on the back. "She's won many prizes at the local fair."

"Oh, Ben's just biased." May smiled, slightly embarrassed at the praise. "So how do you like it here? You bought the Douglas property, didn't you?"

"Yes," Jenny replied, "We love it here; it's like a world of its own."

"It sure is," laughed Ben. "More than you think, I swear time stands still some days."

They all laughed.

"Ben I'll have to get your account number so I can transfer the money for Mustard," said Jack.

"Sure, sure," replied Ben. "Ah I don't know, I'm not big on this cashless business. I miss the old-fashioned greenbacks; I mean there was nothing like having a wad of them in your pocket, it made you feel like a rich man. Soon they'll be stamping a bar code on your hand like a can of baked beans and scanning yer as you walk through the store door," he chuckled. They all laughed but Jack thought it seemed a very familiar scenario, but put it aside for now.

Ben continued, "And what about this economic downturn that's got folks in a spin? I mean, it's not as bad as the great depression but folks are hurtin just the same. The Jepson's place foreclosed last week and the Simmonds are scraping to try to pay their bank mortgage. I'm seeing more and more people going to the church for handouts. Did you know that we now have a deficit into the trillions? What are we doing to the next generation? Heck I'm just grateful that we don't have a mortgage anymore but it doesn't make it any easier for us either, sales are down on both horses and our produce. It just ain't right what's happening to good folk all over the place."

"Oh come, come now Ben," May said gently patting Ben's arm and a little embarrassed at his opinionated outburst. "Jack and Jenny don't want to hear you ranting over the economy. Don't mind Ben he's got his nose into this stuff all the time. Now what have you got in the way of horse riding gear?" May asked quickly changing the subject.

"Umm, well we were all so caught up in the excitement that we haven't had a chance to go and get Sarah a saddle or anything yet, as she was so keen to get here," Jack replied.

"Oh, May probably has something stored out in the shed from her riding instructing days that you can have until you get one specifically for her," Ben said.

"It might be a bit dusty but nothing a good coat of leather conditioner wouldn't fix, come on we'll go take a look," said May.

Jack and May walked out to the barn and left Ben and Jenny still talking at the table. May opened the old wooden barn door and walked towards the back. Jack stood just inside the door his eyes adjusting to the darkness to see hay bales and various farm equipment stored throughout the large old barn. His eyes settled on what looked like an old horse carriage covered in dust and cobwebs, he recognised it from the old photo inside Ben's house.

"Well, this ought to do," May said as she came out from the back of the barn carrying a saddle and noticed Jack staring at the old carriage. "I've told Ben that he should get rid of that old thing, just taking up space - but he won't, sentimental value he keeps telling me, it was his great grandfather's," she explained with a big smile on her face. "It's broken beyond repair, but he still wants to keep it... Men!" she shook her head.

Seth looked at Gabe and raised an eyebrow.

"Not yet, it's not time," said Gabe.

C H A P T E R   F O U R

❝...and so, 'The LORD GAVE AND THE LORD HAS TAKEN AWAY; may the name of the LORD BE PRAISED'..." The Reverend Jim March was in the middle of his Sunday morning sermon, preaching to a congregation of about two hundred and fifty people. Lora was quietly sitting down the front with her mother Bethany, trying not to fall asleep. *I can't wait until this is over,* she thought, *I wonder what Meg's up too, maybe I can catch up with her this afternoon.*

Reverend Jim March, Bethany, and Lora stood by the door, shook hands and made small talk with the congregation as each one walked outside into a beautiful sunny morning. Lora was busting to go home and change out of her dress and find out what Meg was up too.

"Did you enjoy the message?" Jim asked Bethany as they were driving in the car back home.

"Yes, it was wonderful, very well thought out and spoken," she replied with a smile.

Lora took this cue to quickly put on her headphones and pretend she was listening to her music before her father asked her the very same question. Jim looked into the rear-view mirror at his daughter but didn't bother to ask for her response.

Lora got out of the car and ran through the front door up to her room, and changed into her jeans and t-shirt and rang her friend Meg.

"How was church today?" Meg mocked with a giggle.

Lora rolled her eyes and said, "Boring as usual, what are you doing?"

"Well, the fair is in town so I thought I might go down there and check it out. I think Scotty and Ken are going to be there too.

"Okay, I'll be over at your house in five." Lora hung up the phone. "I'm going to Meg's place," she called out to her parents. "Be back this afternoon," she said as she ran out the door.

Jenny was sitting down on the front porch contently watching Sarah groom Mustard. She was talking to him whilst putting plaits in his mane and finishing them off with her own colourful hair baubles. Mustard was enjoying the pampering, his eyelids were low, and he was gradually falling asleep. Jack was down the paddock helping Matthew learn how to ride his motorbike.

"Now this time, go easy on the throttle," she could hear him say after watching Matthew have a near miss with a tree previously.

It was a lovely day, something that they could not have imagined a few months ago. They'd had a good morning, church was great, they'd seen new friends and now were just relaxing and enjoying the afternoon. Evensmore had certainly changed their lives, and Jenny loved it.

Beside her stood her two guardian angels God had assigned to her also contently watching the action in the paddock.

"Looks like they are going to have their hands full," commented one guardian.

They both burst out laughing at the sight of Matthew, once again full throttle and out of control down the paddock with Jack running in hot pursuit after him.

At this instant there was a brilliant flash of light and the Angelic Captain, Jophiel, was standing in front of them. One guardian stiffened to attention prodding the other in the side and motioning to Seth and Gabe to quickly come over and join them.

"Good afternoon sir," they addressed the Captain.

"How is everything here?" Jophiel replied, smiling at all four Guardians standing at attention.

"All is well," they replied.

"Did he see it?" asked Jophiel.

"Yes," replied Seth.

"Well done," said Jophiel. "As you are aware the plan is twofold, Jack must find the truth and then use his position to save many others. It is imperative that the enemy do not become aware of our mission. Do you all understand how important this is to the cause?"

They all nodded.

"Good, as you were." and with that, he was gone.

The smell of hot dogs and fries, mixed with the sound of cheers and screams from the rides had the town fair in full swing. Lora and Meg were taking small bites of their pink cotton candy when two teenage boys, Scotty and Ken came running up behind grabbing them.

"Aaaah, you scared me." Lora laughed at Scotty as he swung her around.

"Hey I'm glad you're here," he said.

"Me too," she said shyly, admiring his handsome features and tousled blonde hair.

The four of them spent an hour laughing and meandering around the fair, taking rides and filling up on hot dogs and candy.

"Hey," said Meg, "I've got an idea." They all looked curiously at her. "Let's get our fortunes told there's a lady here that does them."

"Mm... I don't know Meg," said Lora. "I mean, it sounds kind of scary to me."

"Yeah, I don't know if I'm into that sort of thing," said Scotty warily.

"What can it hurt? Come on who doesn't want to know their future? Besides it's not real, it's just a bit of harmless fun," said Meg.

"Yeah, but I don't know, I've got a bad feeling about that stuff," Lora replied.

"Come on Lora, stop being a goody two shoes there's nothing wrong with it," said Meg as she grabbed Lora's arm and dragged her over into the medium's tent with Scotty and Ken following closely behind.

Inside the tent sat an attractive, middle-aged woman, with her hair half pulled back in a hair clip revealing large hoop earrings and a butterfly tattoo on the nape of her neck. She was busily filing her long crimson nails when she looked up at them.

"Hello darlings," she crooned with a smooth European accent, "are you here for your future telling?"

They nervously looked around at each other when Meg piped up saying, "Yes, we would like our fortunes told please."

"Well, you've come to the right place." She smiled and went on to say, "I am Carla. Who wants to go first?" she asked as she waved her hand.

Meg stepped forward. "Follow me then." She motioned and Meg followed her into the back room of the tent. The others sat down in the chairs and waited.

After 20 minutes Meg burst out into the waiting area, beaming with excitement. "Wow, that was awesome!' "I'm going to marry a handsome, rich, dark-haired man and travel the world, have three kids AND I'm going to live a long, long life."

Lora, Scotty, and Ken sat there nervously smiling at her. "Come on Lora, you've got to go next, there's really nothing to worry about, it's so much fun, you'll love it," Meg said.

Lora got up, took a deep breath and boldly marched into the back room and sat down across the table from Carla. She was trying her best to hide her nerves.

"And what is your name young lady?" Carla asked.

"Um, it's Lora," she replied shyly.

"Aaaaaah... Lora, such a pretty name, let's see what the future holds for young Lora eh!"

Carla laid out the Tarot cards one by one in front of her on the table. Raising her eyebrows and making interesting ooh, and aah sounds at each one she placed down.

In the darkened tent, Lora could not make out the big black hand upon Carla's head with long talons tightly gripping her skull nor could she hear the deep raspy voice speaking deeply into Carla's mind. The monstrous demon with course hair and hunchbacked features was looking at a smaller rough, lizard like demon standing beside Lora.

"Omart, what do you know of this girl?" the big demon rasped to the smaller.

"Well," Omart replied in a high pitch, winy shrill. His spindly arms flailing about animatedly as he spoke. "She's a preacher's daughter, 14-years-old and she goes to Evensmore high. Oh, yeah, she had an aunt who died about six months ago who she was close to. She has a small white dog called Lilly and had a grey cat that passed away two years ago called Toby..." The small demon continued to give the larger one all that he knew about Lora's past and present.

"Tell me more about the aunt... how she died?" the large demon asked.

"It was in a car accident; her name was Mary Jean Baker. Lora gave her a silver heart shaped pendant a few days before the accident. Oh yeah, can you also give her a previous life, you know like an Egyptian princess or something, I love it when you do that," he nervously chuckled.

The large demon resumed his focus, sank his talons deeper into Carla's skull, and began to speak into her psyche.

Carla suddenly stiffened; her eyes became wide, boring deep into Lora's. "Yes, yes I have something for you my child. Your aunt is here with us, ummmm, hang on, M, M, Mmm, Maria, No, No, Mary, Mary is the name that I'm receiving."

Lora stiffened in her chair, and her hands began to wring nervously. Finally, she said, "Is...is she, all right?" her eyes filling with tears.

"Yes, she says that she is fine, that she has passed over to the other side and is enjoying another life peacefully in the universe. She's saying also that it was a quick death and that she did not feel a thing in the car accident. Yes, Yesss, ummmm, she said to tell you that she is still wearing the heart pendant that you gave her for her birthday."

Lora sat astonished and wide-eyed at what she was hearing.

"Also, I am sensing an animal here. A grey cat, he is here with you. The name I'm receiving is T, O, B, Y." She spelt out the letters "Yes that's it, Toby."

"You mean... Toby has been with me all this time?"

"Yes my darling, he has!" She continued, "Mmmm, you are also the daughter of a local preacher but you are unhappy and your soul is searching for the truth. If you keep searching, you will find it my child. Oooooh, hang on one moment… I'm getting that you, my darling were of high importance in a previous life. Aaahh yesss… a princess...an Egyptian princess I believe." Carla smiled and raised her eyebrows to show how impressed she was.

"Wow, how do you know all this about me?"

"I have a gift from the Lord above darling!"

Both demons looked at each other and grinned bearing their fangs.

"More like from OUR Lord below," Omart crackled.

The larger demon maliciously grinned at the other, drool cascading down his jowls. "The fools are easily deceived aren't they," he replied.

CHAPTER FIVE

Now where was that? Jack thought as he sifted through the papers and documents scattered over his desk. Jack had the house to himself, the children had left for school and Jenny had gone into town to get some groceries. "Ah, there it is," he said as he picked up the software requirements documentation. *It'll be in here*, he thought.

Jack skimmed though the pages until his eyes stopped upon a requirement. He slowly read it aloud. "The 'I-Chip' shall be implanted into the subject's right hand." *How did Ben know about this?* he thought, *must have been a lucky guess because all this is classified.* "Mm…interesting!"

The phone rang suddenly and interrupted Jack's thought process. "Hello," Jack answered.

"Hi Jack its Simon, how are things in the country?"

"Great Simon it's really quiet out here, I'm not missing the stress of city life at all."

"That's great, I'm glad it's working out for you. Listen, how's the documentation tracking for the I-Chip project? We have that review next week and I was hoping you were close to finishing it so I can look at it before it goes before the board."

"No problem, I'm actually sending you the last document today for you to look at."

"That's great. Love your work Jack! Okay, well I'll let you get back to it then, talk to you in the review next week."

"Thanks Simon, talk to you then."

Jack hung up the phone and busily got back to tweaking the final draft of the Software Design Document. He had felt a greater degree of pressure on this project than normal because for some reason, there was a rush to push this product out. He really wanted to talk to Jenny about how he was feeling but couldn't because of its Top Secret classification. *I'm on my own on this one,* he thought to himself.

"Hello Jacky, I'm back!" Jenny called as she strove through the door with the groceries in her arms.

Relieved for the distraction he replied, "Hey, you want a hand?"

"Love one!"

Jack marched up the stairs and out the front door to help collect the bags from the car. "You want me to make you a coffee?" he asked.

"Wow, you have become the real house husband, haven't you?"

"Yeah, well I'm just due for one and I really need to take a break." He smiled as he followed her and grabbed two grocery bags.

"Is everything all right?"

"Just work," he said as he walked back inside and turned on the kettle.

"Okay, did everyone print off the first lesson on our study, renewing the mind?" Peter asked. Everyone in the men's bible study nodded their heads in agreement. "Good then, so let's get started. Ted, do you want to read out the first paragraph for us please."

"Do not conform to the pattern of this world, but be transformed by the renewing of your mind. Then you will be able to test and approve

what God's will is—his good, pleasing and perfect will. Romans 12:2."
Ted read the scripture aloud.

"So, what do you think this scripture means?" Peter asked as he looked around at the nine men sitting in the room.

Ted spoke first, "I guess for me it means that I should think on what God would want me to think upon. For instance, instead of dwelling on something negative, like maybe my anger, I should try and focus on self-control and get some scriptures to back it up."

"Excellent, that's a really good example," Peter said. "Jack, have you got something?"

"Well, I know I really don't do this enough, but I think if we want to renew our mind then the best way to do it is by reading the word. Because if we focus on the word then we have the mind of Christ and then we can, like Paul said, 'be able to test and approve what God's will is'."

"Yeah, that's good Jack," said Shaun Barnard. "I know I don't read the word enough but every time I do it does feel like my mind and spirit is being fed, refreshed or something and I'll tend to remember the scriptures later."

The group continued to discuss their thoughts and then broke for supper.

"So, Jack, what projects are you working on?" asked Shaun whilst sipping his coffee.

"Nothing exceptional!" Jack tried to tone it down but seeing Shaun's face made him feel the need to explain his elusiveness a bit further. "Sorry Shaun, but I can't say due to the classification!"

"Ah, so it's some conspiracy, like world domination, or the mark of the beast on our right hand or something?" Ted jested.

Jack looked inquisitively at Ted. "Mark on the hand? You know that's really weird because that's the second time I've heard that in the last month," he exclaimed.

Peter piped up. "The mark of the Beast Jack, in the book of Revelation?"

"Umm sorry, I've been a Christian for two years but I haven't heard of that one," replied Jack. "What am I missing here?"

"Well, Jack, a lot of people don't read the book of Revelation," Peter said.

"Yeah, because most people can't understand it!" laughed Shaun whilst munching on his biscuit.

"Well, yes, it's a bit of a challenge to understand the real meanings behind it and that is primarily why people tend to read the other books instead," Peter added.

"So what's this mark on the hand thing?" Jack asked.

"It's where people are forced to take a mark that represents allegiance with the Antichrist. Anyone who does not have this mark cannot buy or sell and will face persecution and even be put to death. However, God says that anyone who accepts the mark will go to Hell. It's sort of a lose-lose situation," Ted said with a grin.

"Wow, is that really what it says?" asked Jack stunned.

"Yeah, it's in Revelation. The Antichrist will be the head of a one-world government and will take total control over everything, including religion, to the extent that everyone's forced to worship him and not God. But thankfully we are not going to be around to see it, because we are going up," replied Shaun as he pointed heavenward.

"How do you mean?" asked Jack.

"Well, the scriptures say that the church will be taken out before any of this occurs, so we won't go through this persecution. God will remove us before this happens, so we won't be harmed," said Peter.

"Really? Well, that's a relief. It doesn't sound very good," said Jack.

"God revealed this to our two Evensmore preachers, Father Harvey and Father Daniel way back, it's called the secret Rapture. So don't worry, we have nothing to be concerned about, Jesus will return for us before anything like that happens he's definitely going to save his people. Some even say that you can be saved after the secret Rapture too and that we get a second chance if we miss out the first time. So, we really have nothing to worry about, God's not going to let his people suffer through the tribulation," said Shaun confidently.

Jack's Guardians, Seth and Gabe looked at each other. "We wait." Gabe stated.

Seth nodded in agreement.

Jack came home from the bible study and slipped quietly inside the house so he wouldn't disturb his sleeping family. He made himself a hot chocolate, got comfortable on the lounge, opened his bible to the book of Revelation, and began to read. *Well, the first bit is straight forward*, he thought, *it shouldn't be too hard if this is the genre*.

CHAPTER SIX

Peter and Jack sat in the corner table at Betty's Cafe.

"You know, I started to read the book of Revelation the other night after bible study and you were right, it's hard to understand. I mean… I'm not a big fan of fiction writing or Sci-Fi but this is really way out stuff, all these visions et cetera," Jack exclaimed.

"Sure, I know how you feel. That book of the bible is not an easy read but if you keep persisting and re-reading it, it actually starts to become clearer," he replied. "Now before you start, ask the Holy Spirit to help you understand and reveal the things that he wants you to learn right now. He will do it, but be persistent." Peter paused for a moment.

"I guess you could liken it to cleaning a dirty window. At first, all you seem to do is smudge it and make it worse but with more paper towel, cleaner, and elbow grease, the clearer it becomes. Also, don't just look at Revelation, look at the other books as well, a lot of them have references to the end times too."

"Mm, well all right… I'll just stick at it then," he smiled.

"So how do you like it here?" asked Peter.

"We have really settled into this place, it feels like we've always belonged here. The church is so fantastic. I actually want to commend you; we really are getting a lot out of your services."

"It's not me, but the Lord; He's the one who has built it. When I first took over there were only seven of the congregation left in the church. It was bound to be closed; I know one hundred and twenty isn't very big compared to what you're used to, but it's a steady growth."

"Well what I'm used to wasn't exactly cosy; it was big and lacked connection and relationships. But I didn't realise that this little church was on the brink of closure. So how did you turn it around?" Jack asked.

"Well, I believe in stating the truth, straight from the bible. Some preachers like to count their congregation numbers and teach so not to offend, they live in fear of losing their people, and so do everything they can to keep them. Unfortunately, it's become more like a business to them, they want the numbers so they can pay the mortgage and bills so they are careful not to upset anyone; it becomes a vicious circle. However, with this church, I knew God put on my heart to preach the truth, speak out His words, seek Him for what He wants to say to His people and that's exactly what I did. I really had nothing to lose because we only had a small group of people and I just knew God wanted this church to flourish. Slowly but surely it started to grow, people got excited and returned and brought others with them. It was all God, not me."

"Well, you certainly give some profound messages; I mean… it is totally different from where we have come from. I've never really heard the message as strong as you put it, it was more… oh I don't know, I guess, encouragement you know, 'You can do it' mantra style, or drawing from their own experiences and not much of the word coming through and how to overcome and so forth."

Peter chuckled and replied, "Yes, I know what you mean, I've heard *a lot* of those messages myself. No…" Peter paused, "I'm not afraid to lay it on the line and speak about the uncomfortable things people want to ignore or brush over like Hell and the unseen spiritual battle that goes on around us. I ensure that I make it clear in telling the congregation that they need to be fervent in following Christ and not to be slack followers. I guess, at least I will have a clear conscience in knowing that I stood firm in preaching the truth."

"Well, you certainly do! It's like breathing fresh air after so long. I think I was spiritually starving and didn't realise it. I was saved at my previous church; I read the bible at first but have since let the business of life encroach on my time with God." Jack paused and then continued, "I'd hate to admit it but I hardly even pick up my bible now and that's my own doing. I can't blame the church for its lack of teaching; I should be looking after my own spirituality and reading the word myself."

"I'm glad you see it that way." Peter smiled. "But unfortunately, your story is a common one. You see God really convicted me at my last church. Every service there was an alter call given and all that was said was put up your hand if you want to know Christ as your Saviour and then pray this prayer and you're going to Heaven. Well, that was fine, but it just never sat right with me and God kept leading me back to the word to look at scriptures like Matthew 7:21. 'Not everyone who says to me, 'Lord, Lord,' will enter the kingdom of heaven, but only the one who does the will of my Father who is in heaven,' and Matthew 16:24 'Whoever wants to be my disciple must deny themselves and take up their cross and follow me'." Peter stopped before he continued.

"So, I started to question our methods of saving people. Were we just packaging it up to make it sound so easy that you could still live your life as you always have been - there was no real change needed and that it was a sure ticket if you said *Yes*? Because the sad thing was that I would see so many people put up their hand and not have a real *heart change*.

I mean, their character just *wasn't* changing; they were still battling the same demons' years later.

"For instance, they were still struggling with drugs, alcohol, pornography, stealing, committing fornication or still living with their girlfriend or boyfriend, et cetera. I was not seeing any overcomers because they weren't being taught to strengthen their relationship with Christ. They weren't *told* to leave behind their sin or get into God's word or fervently pray for God to help them change and to be dedicated and follow through." Peter looked up to see Jack looking a little perplexed.

"Sorry Jack, let me explain further…you see, when you accept Christ into your heart, your spirit is made new and you become a *new* creation but your soul and body will still try and conduct the same behaviours as before. Your existing behaviour is who you *used* to be, but not who you are *now* with Christ as your Saviour. However, to change your soul and body you have to seek God, read his word to transform your *nature*, but also actively try to stop doing the sin. God will always put the desire in your heart to do this… but it can be deliberately ignored. So that's what I was seeing…" Peter took a long breath before continuing.

"When these people did sin there was simply no remorse, they just continued as they were before and that's what really disturbed me. If people are seeking God they will see a change and when they do make a mistake, *which we all do*, they will earnestly repent, and try harder. That's a heart change."

Gabe and Seth were listening intently. "This is good. This kind of discussion will help strengthen them both." Gabe stated.

"Yes, we need to be watchful; the enemy won't like to hear this." Seth concluded. They both looked at each other and nodded in agreement.

Peter took a breath before he spoke again. "Anyway, there seemed to be more backsliders than overcomers and it broke my heart. So when I came to Evensmore, twelve months ago, I decided that I would be straight about becoming a follower of Christ, so people knew what they had to do, how they had to change, and what they had to look forward to. That's why when someone accepts Christ we talk to them straight away and also encourage them to do our new Christians' course to help start them on their way."

"Well, I can honestly say that I have never heard an alter call quite like yours," Jack said smiling. "You certainly make it clear."

"It's truth," Peter exclaimed. "We do have to deny ourselves and put away the old nature. But what people need to understand is that when you seek first the kingdom of God and be obedient to Him then the blessings will chase you down - you will have the desires of your heart. Therefore, you are not really losing anything but gaining everything, plus eternity. That's why I preach it hard. I mean, if you were to go and buy a car wouldn't you rather the sales person was up front and told you everything about it so you could make an informed and committed decision before purchasing it?"

Jack nodded in agreement.

"Well, it's the same thing, we need to let people know the cost of following Christ, letting the *old* self go but show them that the benefits will and do far outweigh the things we have to leave behind.

Gabe noticed the slight shadowy movement first. Peering through the café window was a small black messenger spirit intently spying on Jack and Peter's conversation. Gabe subtly signalled Seth and drew his attention to the small demon fixatedly gazing through the glass.

Seth coolly moved over towards the café door behind a large pot plant so not to draw any attention, and then with lightning speed he dashed outside, clasped the tiny demon behind the neck, and picked it up.

"W-w-what are you doing?" It squealed in fear.

Seth placed the demon down and spun it around to face him; it flapped its small black wings to regain its balance as Seth drew his regal sword, holding the radiant blade against its slender throat. "No… what are you doing?" Seth demanded.

"N-nothing, I was just passing by and was simply curious."

"About what?"

"Just curious." It smiled a set of misshapen rodent's teeth. Seth pushed his blade a little harder. W-w-wait… I was just listening that's all, nothing bad…just listening."

"Why?" Gabe spoke sternly, now joining the conversation.

"I have no real reason… I-I-I'm just doing my job, you know… I just watch and listen for things."

"What have you heard?"

"Nothing…I heard nothing, they're just talking. Nothing unusual." It smiled meekly.

"You have no business here then," Seth responded, as he dropped his grasp, withdrew his sword, and stepped back letting the spirit go.

The demon immediately took flight, its wings flapping and beating as fast as it could to put as much distance between him and the angels.

Gabe and Seth returned to Jack's side.

I mean…you are a relatively new Christian, tell me how it felt when you accepted Christ." Peter asked.

"It was amazing," Jack exclaimed, "I went from a person who worried and stressed over every little thing. I would strive to get ahead in life, in my career and try to control *all* of my circumstances. It was tiring! But then, when I asked Jesus into my heart…well I can't describe it. It was as… a *weight* was lifted off; I slowly started to feel peace and learnt that God was in control, not me. It didn't come over night… and it was a gradual change, but little by little, I felt that I could trust Him with my circumstances and give my worries over to Him to sort out…and He did. I would never go back Peter; I'm completely a different person now."

"That's the key," Peter said enthusiastically. "Giving over your life to Him so He *can* direct your path, but not all people do this. I mean in Matthew 7:22-23 Jesus states, 'Many will say to me on that day, 'Lord, Lord, did we not prophesy in your name and in your name drive out demons and in your name perform many miracles?' Then I will tell them plainly, 'I never knew you. Away from me, you evildoers'."

Peter hesitated before he continued. "Now that really got me thinking… I thought well, they obviously made a decision for Christ at some stage, because they had that authority by His name to cast out demons and perform miracles, but they never had a relationship with Him. It made me realise that many people who *think* they are going to Heaven will not be. John 15:6 states, 'If you do not remain in me, you are like a branch that is thrown away and withers; such branches are picked up, thrown into the fire and burned'. Further to this, 2 Peter 2:20-21 tells us 'If they have escaped the corruption of the world by knowing our Lord and Savior Jesus Christ and are again entangled in it and are overcome, they are worse off at the end than they were at the beginning. It would have been better for them not to have known the way of righteousness, than to have known it and then to turn their backs on the sacred command that was passed on to them.'

The Book of Peter makes it clear in the scripture that he is talking about Christians who turn away from God and return to their sinful nature. Therefore, it's not a *onetime* prayer thing, it's a life walk. I realised that people were not aware of this; you *can* lose your salvation. So, I decided then that I would teach the congregation the truth... unfortunately it didn't go down well with the senior pastors in my previous church and many of the congregation complained and said that it was too confronting and I should soften my messages. Now what's that telling you?"

"So, what you're saying is that you can pray the sinner's prayer, but you still might not make it to Heaven? Wow, I mean, I thought that once you accepted Christ then you are assured to go to Heaven no matter what!"

"Well no... but I'll explain further." Peter smiled. "It's not 'no matter what', but that's what a lot of preachers are saying too and honestly believe, they say 'once saved always saved', but it's completely false. If you read the scriptures, Jesus makes it quite clear. Take the example of the letter to the Laodiceans in Revelation 3:15-16, 'I know your deeds, that you are neither cold nor hot. I wish you were either one or the other! So, because you are lukewarm—neither hot nor cold—I am about to spit you out of my mouth. Also look at Revelation 3:1-5." Peter opened his bible and read the passage.

'...I know your deeds; you have a reputation of being alive, but you are dead. Wake up! Strengthen what remains and is about to die, for I have found your deeds unfinished in the sight of my God. Remember, therefore, what you have received and heard; hold it fast, and repent. But if you do not wake up, I will come like a thief, and you will not know at what time I will come to you.

Yet you have a few people in Sardis who have not soiled their clothes. They will walk with me, dressed in white, for they are worthy. The one who is victorious will, like them, be dressed in white. I will never blot out the name of that person from the book of life, but will acknowledge that name before my Father and his angels.'

Jack suddenly interrupted Peter. "I will never blot out the name of that person from the book of *life?*" he leant forward exclaiming with a concerned look upon his face. "So, if Jesus is saying here that he won't remove your name, then there's an *implication* that your name *can* be removed? This is scary!" Jack shook his head and leant back.

"Yes, I can see you are realising the enormity of this. Many people are unaware of this possibility. It's a fact and it is stated quite clearly."

"So, these churches Jesus is writing to, they are Christ followers?" Jack asked.

"Yes definitely, they once were fervent for Christ but then became lukewarm; they became spiritually dead, not seeking God's presence. In 1 John 2:4, Jesus said that 'whoever says, 'I know him,' but does not do what He commands is a liar, and the truth is not in that person.' Now where do liars go?" Peter asked before he continued. "I'm telling you that lukewarm is just not acceptable. Yet many people go through their Christian lives being lukewarm for Christ. You can't be half a disciple and God makes that clear in his word. I'm afraid that many people who claim to be Christians will not be going to Heaven."

"Really? You've got me quite concerned," Jack replied.

"Please, don't get me wrong Jack. There is God's grace and he will cover our sins and mistakes if we earnestly repent, but if you are not trying to follow Christ, like trusting Him with your life and decisions, reading His word, seeking His presence and asking for forgiveness if you do sin. But just simply going to church on Sunday, singing a few praise songs and then living your life like you used to before you were saved, then I have to really question your salvation. Jesus is clear that not all people who think they are saved will be *saved*. This really concerns me because there are many Christians who are living their lives thinking that God's grace will cover them always and that they have a one-way ticket to Heaven. I think that people feel that they *can't* lose their salvation no matter what. It's definitely not so! Each one of us must actively be seeking and pursuing God's Will. The church desperately needs to return to the first love like it states in Revelation 2:4."

Jack was pondering everything that Peter explained before he admitted, "It makes me realise that I've been so slack in reading the word and spending time with God. I really need to wake up to myself and take this seriously."

"Good," Gabe exclaimed. He and Seth were still listening attentively to what Jack was saying and were excited that he was now understanding what it really meant to follow the King.

"This is the start, we must continue to encourage him to seek the truth," Seth stated. "However, we must watch out for him, the enemy will not like where he is heading."

"You *must* take this seriously." Peter paused. "No one can afford to be lukewarm! I guess Jack, it's like this… you have met me, but don't really *know* me yet. The only way to know someone is to spend time with them and to form a relationship. It's the same with God, you can ask Him into your heart, but if you do not seek to fellowship with Him and know His ways, read His word and actively obey Him, then you do not have a relationship with Him, just an introduction to Him. We cannot go through our whole lives thinking that everything will be fine and God will just allow us into Heaven because of *one* prayer that we've long since forgotten. There needs to be that heart change and a pursuit for God." Peter took a breath before he continued on another train of thought. "I think many Christians don't realise what can hold you back in your God walk, I mean, a good example is harbouring un-forgiveness. Now this is something that will stop you entering the kingdom, it states it clearly in Matthew 18:21-35 where He tells a parable about the king rescinding his servant's debt because the servant didn't forgive another. I have actually seen countless people come to church, who have been hurt by others, and are still hanging on to this resentment. This will stop them going to Heaven if they don't deal with it and repent." Peter paused sensing the concern in Jack; he thought it best to shift the subject to a much lighter tone. "So... How is your family?" he smiled.

"They're great." Jack lit up again. "Sarah just loves her new pony, Mustard, and Matthew is mastering his motor bike. Every Saturday we lead Mustard and Sarah over to Ben and May's to get her riding lessons. Matthew follows on his bike and Ben gets on his quad bike and they ride all over the property, it's good to see them enjoying the country life. I'm going to get a motor bike myself."

"The Jacksons are lovely people," Peter stated.

"Do they go to church?"

"They go to Reverend March's church down on South Street."

"Oh, I wasn't sure and I didn't feel comfortable enough to ask Ben what they believed."

"Yeah, Ben's a stickler for tradition, most of his generation went to that church, but I don't know where he is at with his faith. I have sat in one of Reverend March's sermons and it is quite different to mine." Peter left it at that.

"Ben really knows his stuff about what's happening to the world economy," Jack said.

"He sure does." Peter chuckled and continued explaining, "And rightly so, as a lot of people want to stick their head in the sand and ignore what's going on around them. A lot of people are in trouble, we have had a huge increase in handouts of food and bill vouchers just this past few months. But God is still in control and He knows what's going on, we just have to help those who are in need."

Jack looked at his watch. "Ah, Sorry Peter, I'm going to have to go, I promised Jenny I would be back for when the children got home, she's playing tennis this afternoon. Thanks so much for the chat and coffee," he said as he rose to leave. "Hey would you like to come over for dinner this Friday night? I'll check with Jenny to see if it's fine but I'm sure it would be."

"I would love to, thanks," Peter replied.

"Okay great I'll call you to confirm details then." Jack smiled as he turned and left the cafe.

CHAPTER SEVEN

"Do another princess one!" the demon Rebellion said to Crystalyn.

"Shhhhh, I *KNOW* what I am doing, so shut up and let me do it," he snapped back as he probed Lora's sleeping head with his long, silvery thin talons. "She will believe, I just have to go slowly, it works every time!"

Rebellion grinned, a slimy mouthful of sharp yellowing fangs, his eagerness nearly getting him slapped. These two were delighting in twisting Lora's thoughts into believing what they were telling her. Their malicious minds were intertwining with hers to control her thinking.

Lora tossed and turned in her fitful sleep, making small muffled noises, her body occasionally twitching sharply as if she was running, escaping in her dreams.

The two demons just grinned at each other as they continued their night's work.

Everyone was asleep in Jack's house, except for Jack; he too had been tossing and turning unable to sleep soundly. Gabe and Seth stood casually nearby watching Jack as he tossed and turned, they both felt the presence of the Holy Spirit moving around Jack urging him to get up and read God's word. They both waited patiently until Jack gave in and quietly grabbed his bible off the bedside table and crept out into the lounge room.

"Finally!" Seth said to Gabe as they followed him out of the bedroom.

Jack sat for a while contemplating his conversation with Peter. He prayed,

"Father, please forgive me for my lack of conviction to your cause, I desperately want to be fervent in seeking your will for my life. I'm so sorry for not reading your word, praising, and praying regularly. I ask for your forgiveness for any sins that I have committed, I also willingly forgive anyone who wronged me. Thank you for saving me and choosing me to be your own, please help me to love people and be passionate for sharing your message of salvation. Amen."

Jack flipped open his bible. "Okay, here we go again... Revelation," Jack mumbled to himself and prayed again, "Lord, please reveal what you want me to see in your word tonight; please give me wisdom and knowledge to be able to understand your teachings, I ask that your Holy Spirit guides me. Thank you in the name of Jesus, Amen."

Jack opened his bible, found the book of Revelation, and started to read. He came to Revelation 3:5. "Ah, that's what Peter was talking about... mmm it does seem that your name could possibly be removed." He pondered this and continued on reading, trying to take in the words on each page. Seth stood nearby, his countenance started to glow as he was prompted by the Holy Spirit. He waited until Jack was near a certain passage and he reached out and touched Revelation 13:16 with his sword and made the words literally glow and jump out off the page at Jack. "He also forced everyone, small and great, rich and poor, free and slave, to receive a mark on his right hand or on his forehead." Jack read the words aloud slowly, taking each one in.

"WOAH! What? Hang on, right hand or forehead?" he said as he re-read the passage again. "This can't be right, is this it, is this the mark?" He jumped up off the lounge and started pacing his thoughts reeling with realisation; *Oh No, this can't be right.* He sat back down and re-read the passage over again as well as the next verse, slowly regaining his thoughts. *This must be a mistake*, he said to himself, re-reading the passage once again. *It can't be coincidental surely. Does this mean I'm involved in creating the mark of the beast? Is this what I've been working on? No, surely not!* He continued to whisper out loud trying to make sense of his thoughts.

Seth and Gabe looked on and waited.

"This is the beginning of Jack's journey," Gabe stated. "He *must* fulfil what God has called him to do."

Jack got up and started pacing again, rubbing his head with his hands, moving around the lounge room, a twisting knot was starting to form in his stomach as he was trying to take in this revelation. *This can't be true, surely, maybe it's something else, maybe I'm not really working on this stuff, I mean this is too soon and this Revelation passage is way off into the future, I mean we are not even supposed to be here when this happens.* He paced the floor, mumbling aloud to himself, *it's got to be just coincidental.*

Jack went into the kitchen and made himself a hot chocolate, but could not shake this feeling of trepidation that lingered over him. *Oh, God, what if it's true, what if I am creating the very thing that will make millions suffer...the creation of the enemy's mark? Lord, help me, give me wisdom, what do I do?* Jack felt sick, his stomach felt like it had twisted around like a wet wringing towel, and he started to feel the pain of the acid and bile rise in his throat with each worrisome thought.

Seth and Gabe stood by and watched Jack in his emotional turmoil. "Let him be for now," Gabe said. "The Lord will reveal to him what needs to be done."

Seth responded with a nod of agreement.

Daylight started to break to reveal a beautiful Friday morning. The sun was rising with its light rays streaking orange and red hued ribbons across the morning sky and the birds were twittering and singing choruses to bring in the new day. However, Jack was still sitting in the lounge, his tired listless eyes fixed on the passage in the bible. His thoughts dulled to a feeling of overwhelming guilt and hopelessness.

"Hey Meg." Lora waved as she ran towards her best friend.

"Hey, did you finally do your math?" Meg asked.

"Yeah, it was boring but I finished it late last night," Lora replied as they both walked into class.

"I didn't finish mine," Meg cringed.

"Ah no Meg, not again, Mrs Pempie is really going to get mad at you, this is the third time now."

"I know, I know, I got watching TV, I'll just have to come up with another excuse. Maybe you could distract her or something." She looked pleadingly at her friend.

"I'll think of something." Lora shook her head in empathy.

"Okay settle down." The high school teacher, Mrs Pempie, raised her voice over the noise of the students' babble. "I want you to open your textbooks, and I'll walk around and take a look at the exercises I gave you to complete."

"Excuse me Mrs Pempie," Lora piped up in amongst the frenzy of students opening their texts. "I was wondering if we could go over exercise 16, 17, and 18 in the text as I really struggled with that."

"Yes, that will be fine Lora... who else wants to go over these?" There was a show of hands.

Meg mouthed the words, "Thank you."

Lora grinned.

"That was a lovely meal Jenny," said Peter. "Thank you so much. It's been a long time since I've had such a nice home cooked dinner. Jude used to be a great cook, I suspect the Lord has her in the kitchen whipping up something as we speak," he chuckled as he and Jenny walked into the lounge room to sit down with their coffees.

"How long has it been?" Jenny asked.

"Jude passed away just over 11 years ago now, I do miss her greatly, and we were best friends. She was only 48 at the time."

"Wow, so young," Jenny replied.

"Yes, it was young and I went through a real stage of being angry with God, but I know God doesn't bring death. We live in the enemy's world. I look back now and know that we didn't have a healthy lifestyle. We were both very overweight, we ate the wrong things like take away, fried, overcooked food, and enjoyed our sugary drinks and cakes and we didn't exercise. The bible clearly states to look after your temple and we weren't, eventually the body gives in to disease, it's not God's fault but our very own doing. It's our responsibility to look after ourselves and live healthy. I see so many people come crying to God to heal them from diseases that could have been preventable if they had just looked after themselves. So now I try to eat a healthy diet of fresh fruit, vegetables, juices, meat and fish. I try to stay away from sugar and have a small amount of carbs, and I exercise for at least half hour each day. I try to incorporate many raw foods into my meals and I feel like I'm 20 years old again. It's just a pity that Jude wasn't with me to enjoy it fully."

"You didn't want to remarry?" Jenny asked.

"No… no one could replace my Judy, I'm sure I could of but I don't have the desire to. I have my son and daughter and now I have two grandchildren, so I'm content."

"They're asleep!" Jack said as he came downstairs and joined Peter and Jenny.

"What's wrong Jack? You're not yourself tonight," Peter inquired.

Jenny looked up at Jack and raised one eyebrow, Jack sat down next to Jenny in the sofa picked up his coffee and took a few sips and gathered his thoughts. "Well, you know that I'm currently working on a major project at the moment that is highly classified."

"Yes, you've mentioned that previously."

"Okay well, I really need to talk to you but I'm torn between confidentiality and honesty."

"How do you mean?"

"Meaning I could get fired, lose all credibility, get the pants sued off of me and go to jail if I tell anyone about this information."

"Mmm, well I see your dilemma then. Have you sought the Lord about telling me?"

"Yes, and I feel that he is directing me to talk to you."

"Well you know that it would be strictly between you and me Jack, I'm not going to talk to anyone else about what you are wanting to discuss, and besides I have obligations to privacy as well."

"I've told Jenny," Jack said, as he looked over to her sitting beside him on the couch. "I couldn't keep quiet any longer, it's just consuming me." Jack sat there anxiously wringing his hands, looking towards the floor.

"I've been working on this project since conception," he continued. "I mean, I was the one who came up with the initial concept. We all thought it was a brilliant idea; the customer was over the moon at its simplicity, technology and the problems that it could solve. I was the shining star on this one so they let me run with it. I spent countless hours, fleshing out requirements and researching new technological advances. I was being paid a bomb as the Engineering Lead and they kept bumping up my salary, as the customer was so happy with my work. I had some of the top R&D professionals assigned to me to gather any information that I required. I didn't realise how immense the customer's corporation was but they were paying us big money to pursue this and bring it to fruition quickly.

"But I didn't know Peter, I just didn't realise, how could I? But I should have known; I mean I started looking at this concept two and a half years ago, just before I became a Christian. So why didn't God tell me not to do it, or to stop, why didn't someone let me know?" Jack held his head in his hands shaking his head, looking up helplessly at Peter. Jenny had her arm around him with tears in her eyes, never seeing her husband this distraught before.

"What do you mean Jack, you're losing me." Peter looked confused.

"Peter, it's the mark... the mark of the beast, the one mentioned in Revelation."

"How do you know?"

Jack knowingly chuckled to himself and shook his head. "Oh, I know because I know this project like the back of my hand... no pun intended. I wrote it and created it and it is already in testing as we speak. They rushed this one through, as I've never seen before. I was so excited about it because it was like my very own baby being birthed into the world. It's a brand-new advancement, which meant also for me that I too would become a sort after prize possession, so it was a real win-win for both parties."

"Sooo... what you're saying is that you have created the mark of the beast?" Peter said slowly, thinking about his question.

"Yes, the one mentioned in Revelation."

"Okay...so what exactly makes you think that this thing... this concept you're working on is the mark?"

"Well, firstly it looks so simple, innocent even, and to me it was, it was a way to solve the problems in the world. It's a brilliant idea that would mean that our world is a safer place. Besides the concept isn't entirely new, we have been using this technology on our pets and livestock to keep track of them. So I took a step further and applied the concept to human life."

"Right...go on."

"Well, we have so many problems in the world... like identity theft, monetary funds being stolen, credit cards, bank cards, licenses, or passports being lost or taken. This was the initial concern for our customer, but I took it further and suggested its use to find people who have gone missing - children, the elderly, our armed forces, criminal tracking, identification, keyless entries. Also, for information storage, such as medications and health which is brilliant for those who are unable to talk for themselves. There are numerous things that it is useful for, and I was completely thinking of helping our nation with safety, law enforcement, security, and justice. With the technology we have now, our satellite could track anyone, I mean if I had this implant I could be doing

140 miles per hour in a 40 zone and get pinned for it via the satellite. I could even start my own car or unlock my house door with my hand."

"You said implant; I thought you meant a mark?"

"No, sorry it's an implant, a very tiny microchip."

"But the bible definitely says a mark."

"Well then, so would John have known what a microchip was back then?" Jack looked questioningly at Peter.

"Yes, I see your point."

Two black messenger demons where in hiding, crouching low in silence behind the TV cabinet, intently listening to the conversation. They weren't happy, "Not good, we must get word to the Master." one said to the other.

Jack continued. "Revelation says that no one can buy or sell unless they have this mark. They're not going to tattoo a number on your hand or forehead, that's way too primitive, there's no need with the technology that we have now. It's designed for convenience and speed. For instance, when you go to a grocery store cash register you will get your hand scanned and the amount will come straight out of your bank account, as it does now with your card. This replaces all cards. Its genius! However, it also means that if the implant is enforced and people refuse to have it then they will not be able to buy and sell without it. Just like cash is now - useless. Do you see where my concern is Peter? Do you understand the parallel with the passage in Revelation? It is way too close for my comfort; it's got to be it."

"Yes, I see," Peter said as he pondered his next question and silently prayed for God's wisdom. The Holy Spirit was ministering to him and he could feel it. Jack and Jenny sat there in silence with Jack occasionally looking downward and wringing his hands in turmoil.

"I have this on my shoulders," Jack said as he looked up with tears in his eyes and his brow deeply furrowed, his emotions overcame him. "What have I done, I have aided the enemy of God, I have been his tool to bring this into realisation. I never thought of it being enforced upon people. I have created the very thing that could destroy millions of lives." Jack started to sob, placing his head in his hands, his body shaking and letting out deep cries of anguish. "I have to quit, I have to tell them I'm off the project." Jenny started to cry also, seeing him in this state, holding Jack as wet tears flowed down their faces.

Peter let them go for a few minutes and sat in silence waiting until he felt a prompting from the Holy Spirit. He moved closer in front of them both and made them look at him. "Jack," he said, "don't you think that God knew this?" Jack looked at Peter questioningly but said nothing. "Don't you think that this was a part of God's plan? It is written, it's in front of you in the book of Revelation, and God himself wrote it. So why not you Jack? Why wouldn't God use one of his very own children to create this? If it was not you, it would have been someone else. If God hadn't wanted you to do this he would have got you out of it whether you liked it or not."

Jack looked at Peter. "Do you think so?"

"Yes Jack, I *KNOW* so! Have you read the book of Esther?"

"No."

"Well, this is sort of reminding me of that story, you might want to read it sometime. I won't go into detail but I think, who knows, maybe it was for a time such as this that you were placed into that project."

"I don't understand," Jack replied.

"You will when you read Esther. Don't do anything rash; do not quit your job. I will seek God on this and I want you both to do the same okay. But don't go letting the guilt of the world fall upon your shoulders there is no need. This is God's story and His plan; He knew all along what your destiny was. You have a calling on your life Jack, a big one. I knew that the day I met you. I'm not sure yet what it is but God is going to reveal it to you very soon. Get into the word, pray, wait upon God and trust that He has everything in control okay?"

"Okay," Jack replied hesitantly and clearly unconvinced.

"Jenny?" Peter looked at her and asked.

"Yes, we will," she said.

"Okay, let's pray!"

"Let's go," one demon hurriedly whispered in a faint raspy voice. "We *must* warn the Master." The two messenger demons quietly started to creep out from behind the cabinet.

Seth and Gabe suddenly both heard the scraping sounds of long talons on the floorboards along with the rustling of leathery wings. They knew instantly what the sound was as they spun around and dived, catching the two demons by surprise. They both pinned them tightly with their swords against their chests.

"These two *must* be vanquished; they have heard the conversation and will warn the others. We cannot afford *this* plan to be discovered." Gabe stated.

Seth agreed as they quickly plunged their swords into the two screaming black demons, finishing them off.

CHAPTER NINE

L ora and Meg sat quietly in the schoolyard under a tree eating their lunch.

"Hey, Meg, I'm having some really weird dreams lately, ever since we went and saw that fortune lady at the fair," Lora said.

"Yeah? Like what?" Meg replied inquisitively.

"Well, you know how she said that I used to be this princess in another life?"

"Yeah."

"It's all about that, like I'm there, living and doing what the Egyptians do, it's just really weird and I'm not sure if I like it."

"I think it would be cool, I wish I had a past life. I mean you're learning how they live, what they did I guess. I'm not sure if it's real though, it's probably just dreams. I wouldn't worry about it."

"Yeah, I guess, but the thing is that the other night there was this girl in my dreams and she was telling me that she was my best friend in that time. She too was dressed as a princess."

"WOW! What did she say?"

"Well, she was saying that I actually died when I was 17 years old and that she is so happy to see me again. It's weird. Oh yeah and she said she wanted to meet with me again. It's sort of freaking me out."

"Hey go with it, it sounds like fun, what can it hurt, besides, it's not real they're just dreams. Just say that you want to meet with her and see where it goes. My mum knows a bit about this stuff, she said her grandmother used to be into it, I'll ask her if you like. Just don't tell your dad though," she chuckled.

"Yeah, that would freak him right out." Lora smiled.

Crystalyn and Rebellion sat there attentively listening to every word the girls were saying. "Nice work," Rebellion said.

"I told you slow and steady reels them in. They are so predictable!" Crystalyn replied. They both looked at each other and started to chuckle bearing their sharp yellow fangs, red eyes squinting as their black wings were unfurling and shaking with each rumble.

Jack was still not right in his emotions; he hadn't slept properly for weeks. He looked like a wreck, he was having bad headaches, his eyes were bloodshot, and he hadn't shaved. He sat quietly at his desk but couldn't work; his heart wasn't in it anymore. There was no drive, no more excitement just pure dread. "What am I going to do?" he said aloud with his head in his hands.

Gabe and Seth stood nearby, their hearts going out to Jack seeing him in his turmoil. As Jack sat silently in his chair, Gabe leaned over to him and whispered, "Just pray Jack, pray." Jack breathed out a sigh and then started to whisper a very soft, faint prayer, but then stopped in silence.

"Pray Jack, come on," Seth said softly.

But Jack said nothing.

"How was school today Lora?" Jim asked as they sat at the dinner table.

"Fine," she replied.

"Are you keeping up with your school work?"

"Yes," Lora said as she secretly rolled her eyes and shovelled more potato mash into her mouth.

"That's good, because your studies are very important if you aim to get anywhere in this world."

Whilst her parents talked, Lora continued to eat her dinner quickly so she could leave the table and get up to her room and away from her boring father.

"May I be excused please?" she asked politely.

"Sure," Bethany replied, "just leave your plate on the sink darling; I'll clean it up for you."

With that, she was bounding up the stairs into her room. *Finally*, she thought, *A bit of peace and quiet. Man, why do I have to have such a stiff, old fashioned, boring family? It drives me crazy sometimes. Maybe I'll just go to bed early and try to meet Crystalyn tonight.* Lora read some of her book then switched off the light. As soon as her head hit the pillow she was asleep dreaming.

In her dream she saw many rooms in which she assumed to be a huge palace - she looked at her clothes. She was wearing a tight-fitting light blue dress like an under slip with thin straps over the shoulders, it reached down to her ankles and it felt very soft and flowing. She felt the weight of the chunky jewellery around her neck and her dark hair softly falling down around her shoulders. *This feels so real* she thought.

"Ana!" she heard someone shout, "Ana, you came back." She looked around to where the voice was coming from and it was Crystalyn, the princess girl she had met previously in her dreams. Crystalyn wore a soft white flowing dress with a large yellow sash around her waist. Her hair was jet black and straight with a gold band around her forehead. Her eyes were the deepest green with thick black kohl eyeliner, her lips were bright red, and she wore a magnificent golden and red gemstone collar around her neck. She was beautiful. "Ana, I thought you would not return I have waited for you," she said.

"I don't understand, my name is Lora… not Ana," Lora replied.

"In your world you may be Lora, to me you will always be my best friend Ana… but I can call you Lora if you wish?"

"Yes please, it's too confusing," Lora responded meekly.

"We have much to catch up on, come on let's go out to the garden." On saying that Crystalyn grabbed Lora's hand and lead her outside into the beautiful sunlit garden. They sat near a clear blue pool.

"You said I died when I was 17?" Lora asked.

"Yes, you drowned, just here in this pool," Crystalyn said.

"How? Couldn't I swim?"

Crystalyn laughed and replied, "Yes silly, you could swim very well. I'm not sure how, but your father found you here lying face down afloat. Your father was heartbroken. Oh, how I've missed you, it hasn't been the same since. I'm so glad you're back, we can now live together free in the universal conscience."

CHAPTER TEN

Tuesday

"Hey Peter," Jack said, "thanks for coming over."

"No problem. How are you feeling?" Peter looked at him shocked at his dishevelled appearance.

"I have written my resignation."

"No...Jack?" Peter said in shock.

"I just can't do this any longer. I mean every phone call, and meeting, I can't shake the feeling that I want out. Some days I feel physically sick just thinking about it. I really don't think I can do this Pete! What if this is God's way of telling me to leave it," Jack responded worried.

"Is that what you're really sensing or is this your head talking?"

"Maybe it's my head," Jack paused. "But I don't know what I'm thinking, I feel so torn. I can't tell if it's God or me. One minute I feel that I *can* do this and the next I'm doubled over with anxiousness. I mean what is that telling you? It can't be right....Right?"

"Listen, God will not give you something that he hasn't equipped you for. He is always with you to guide and help you fulfil His will for your life."

"How do I know it's His will and not just a massive mistake? That

I've gone off track on my own tangent and created something I thought would be awesome, but is actually devastating…how do I know?"

"You know deep down. Listen to your heart not to what your head is telling you. Get your emotions out of it. I know you want to run and leave this behind you, but, how can you? I know you Jack, if you left now you would always wonder."

"Would I…really? I think I would feel relieved! Anyway… why me? Why would God have me invent this, thinking that I was changing the world for good and it turns out that it's the opposite?"

"No, you wouldn't feel relieved; you're not made like that. God created you for this, you may not see it, but I *know* in my heart that it's right. I've said it before, why *not* you? It was going to happen anyway, whether it was you or someone else. Think about that. Do you really know why God has placed you in this situation? I mean, come on Jack, who better placed than someone who knows the system intimately, who designed and built it, who knows its capabilities… along with its flaws?"

"I don't know I just don't see how it can be what I'm supposed to be doing. I really think I should resign and leave this all behind me."

Gabe looked at Seth concerned and said, "He must not quit."

Seth paused for a moment before walking over to Peter and touched him gently on the shoulder, speaking into his spirit coaxing him to continue to help encourage Jack to stay.

"Okay," Peter continued, "I fully understand what you're saying but let me tell you this. We have such a short time here on earth; this time is like an interview for our eternity, so what we do here on earth counts. Sure, we can become a Christian and go to Heaven, but I want a 'well done good and faithful servant' statement when I greet Jesus." Peter paused momentarily and changed his tact. "Jack did you know that there are rewards and a hierarchy in Heaven?"

"No."

"Well, there is, and these high positions are not reserved for only people who are preachers or… volunteer aid workers, it's for those who fulfil their calling on their lives. Paul says in 1 Corinthians 9:24 'Do you not know that in a race all the runners run, but only one gets the prize? Run in such a way as to get the prize'. So run your race to win.' And the last part of 1 Corinthians 9:25 says '... but we do it to get a crown that will last forever'."

Peter continued, "So this means that we all have our *own* race to run, Jesus didn't call us to *all* be preachers or like Mother Teresa. Each of us has an individual purpose; God places this on our lives. For instance, for one person it may be to be a great wife to her husband, mother to her children and to raise them in a Godly way. For another it may be to become a businessperson and help fund the kingdom of God, or to adopt orphans, or become a teacher or a movie star and affect the film industry. It's individual, and God will show each one of us what He wants for our lives. However, we can hinder this with our own will, our own wants, or fears. We may not get the rewards in Heaven that we would have received if we had followed our calling. I think people get confused and assume that the Pastors or missionaries will get the greatest rewards, but it's not so. Those who achieve their individual calling will get the rewards."

Peter took a deep breath before he made his next point. "Jack, God is making it very clear to you that *this* is where He wants you right now, so please do not listen to doubt or fear because it could affect your calling. It is crucial at this point in time that you stay the course and complete what God has asked you to do. Because you actually don't know why He has you in this position, what if it's to do something great for His people?" He paused looking solemn. "For I believe that if you intentionally refuse what God has called you to do then it is the sin of disobedience. Matthew 7:21 clearly states, 'Not everyone who says to me, 'Lord, Lord,' will enter the kingdom of Heaven, but only the one who does the will of my Father who is in heaven', Jack please don't reject what God has asked of you."

"I see what you're saying," Jack said with emotion, "but how do I know that *this* is where I'm supposed to be? I have so much doubt, and I'm afraid that you are right…fear."

"You need to press into God and get the answer for yourself, I can't convince you, no one can… you have to get this from God. Promise me that you will stop the turmoil and indecisiveness and simply go to God for the answer. Your future is riding on it."

"I will."

That night, Peter sat quietly in his lounge chair and prayed for his friend, hoping that he had taken his advice.

The angels also hoped that Jack had listened. They looked at each other, "He cannot falter… for this is hinging upon him," said Seth firmly.

"So you're telling me that this stuff could be real?" Meg asked.

"Yes Meg, I mean, really real," Lora replied.

"Mm, well, I did ask my mum and she said that she used to play around with it but didn't take it seriously. She told me that it wasn't real, just pretend and it's really only your imagination."

"Well, I think it's real. It feels real and it's getting *more real* to me. I go there every night now and Crystalyn and I, we are such good friends, like you and me Meg. I can tell her everything."

"So you now have two best friends, one real one and one imaginary," Meg chided, but a little jealous.

"Meg you're my number one friend and Crystalyn… well, I don't think it's just in my head. Why don't you try it and see for yourself?"

"How am I going to do that? I can't just make up someone; I don't have a vivid imagination like you do Lora."

"Well, I don't know then. I guess…maybe just ask for a friend before you go to bed or something, maybe it will just happen."

"Maybe," Meg replied, but she was not keen about the idea.

Wednesday

Jack had pondered what Pete had said, he had looked up the scriptures and spent time alone in his office, not doing work but simply sitting quietly and reassessing everything. However, he struggled to shake the ominous feeling of guilt that hovered over him like a persistent vulture. He decided to re-read his resignation letter.

Gabe and Seth stood beside him looking concerned at what Jack was contemplating.

They stood by and watched as he tweaked some wording then moved the mouse curser over the 'Send' button on his email. Jack hesitated.

Gabe quickly glanced at Seth and slowly shook his head, as he said, "No… don't do this Jack."

Seth moved swiftly, his sword alighted with fire as he plunged the blade into the wireless router at the very moment Jack went to hit 'Send.'

Jack suddenly saw the words 'Internet connection is down' appear on his computer screen. "Oh great, my day just gets better." He said despondently as he got up to check the router. He sat there for a further 10 minutes trouble shooting the error before giving up and going downstairs into the lounge room.

Seth removed his sword from the router and they both followed Jack. They watched as Jack picked up his bible. Seth prodded. "Pray Jack, you will get the answer you need, just pray."

Jack felt the prompting and his lips began to move, "Father, I feel so terrible and so guilty for what I have done. I feel helpless and stuck. I need you to guide my steps, to give me strength and help me continue. I can't do this without you. I need you more now than I ever have. I have unknowingly created something that will adversely change the world, I feel like I'm sending people to their death. Please help me God, please come to me, and give me direction. Show me your will because I'm so, so lost and don't understand. I need you to tell me if I'm to *stay* or to *leave*, please help me...just help me God."

As Jack sat there, he couldn't physically see the results of his prayer at work and the many iridescent angels who were dropping down into his room, ministering to him, giving him comfort, peace, and imparting wisdom and strength. Their massive wings were enveloping him, their glory radiating and emanating through Jack's body. Jack just sat quietly in silence waiting. Slowly he could feel a sensation flowing through him, a shift in his emotions, strengthening but also calmness and peace that he had never experienced. Then clear strong words broke through, a stirring deep within his heart, as he had never felt before. He listened and he heard.

"I love you Jack. My ways are not your ways. Just trust in me and *stay*." Proverbs 3:5.

"Proverbs 3:5, Proverbs 3:5," he constantly repeated as he picked up his bible and quickly opened it to the passage.

"Trust in the Lord with all your heart and lean not on your own understanding," he read. "Wow, I think I just heard from God." His excitement and joy rising as he kept re-reading the passage. "Okay Lord, I've heard you… I'll stay! Thank you, Father. Hey Jenny," he called.

Jenny came racing in from the kitchen calling, "What's wrong?"

"Not wrong, but right. I just heard God speak to me," Jack said in his excitement.

"What? How?"

"I know, it's amazing, I've never had this happen before, maybe because I have never given Him the chance and listened. But I did and it was so clear, like someone just spoke right into me…right through me even." Jack was speaking a million miles an hour expressing his excitement.

"Well, what did He say?" she said excitedly.

"He told me that He loved me, to trust Him and to stay, and then I got this scripture. Look here it is," talking elatedly as he pointed to the passage in the bible.

"Wow, that's awesome, and Jack you look different, lighter or something." Jenny looked at his face.

"I am Jen, I feel it, I know now that God is in control of this situation, there are no coincidences, and I *am* in His will. It's such a relief, I feel like a weight has been lifted off me, and you know what the exciting part is?"

"What?" She smiled.

"Finding out what He has in store for us."

CHAPTER ELEVEN

Friday

"Thank you," Jack said with a smile as the waitress at Betty's Cafe put the two lattés in front of Jack and Peter.

"Well, you're looking better. I have to admit I was very worried about you. You looked terrible." Peter smiled.

"Thanks Pete," Jack chuckled, "I do feel much better… but I still have my occasional moments where doubt creeps in."

"I've been praying that God would give you some direction."

"Well it worked. He has." Jack beamed.

"And?"

"I took your advice and prayed about it, I had an amazing experience. I heard God tell me to stay." Jack grinned. "But that still doesn't make me feel comfortable about the whole idea. My head is still telling me to leave."

"That just sounds like fear. I've learnt always go with the last thing God told me. If he said stay… then stay." He smiled reassuringly.

"Thanks for your advice." Jack continued, feeling a renewed sense of clarity. "I guess now I'm starting to look at it this way. It may not be the actual I-Chip itself, but what it represents. I mean once everyone has the implant then how much easier is it to enforce a one world government regime and religion. All money will be electronic and if you don't have the I-Chip then you can't buy or sell, no one will accept any other form of currency. They could easily just wipe your bank funds to zero and you couldn't do anything about it."

"So you think it's still the mark?"

"Maybe not the I-Chip itself... I mean... what may happen is that the Antichrist will request everyone to add another number to their personal identification on the chip to verify that they are in allegiance to him. For instance...I don't know... your I-Chip ID may be 12345 then if you accept the mark, they add the 666 on the end of your ID or something. I'm really not sure but I do feel the I-Chip will be the vessel in which it is enforced."

"Yes, you could be right, but our hope is that we, the saints will not have to endure."

"Mm, I hope so because this thing is going full steam ahead Peter. We already have families volunteering to be the first to receive it, I mean they can't wait."

"Really?"

"Yes!" Jack paused and quickly changed the subject, as he didn't want to think any further about it. "But, on a lighter note, well, I've really been studying, I mean like never before. God has given me this, umm I don't know, an unquenchable thirst to get into His word. I keep having this urge to read about the end times, the book of Revelation and other scriptures related to the return of Jesus."

"That's great!"

"Well, I have a question for you; I can't actually find where in the bible it says that the church will be taken out before the Antichrist takes control. I've looked repeatedly and maybe I'm just missing it completely,

I mean it must be in there for people to believe it right?"

"Well, actually there is no scripture that specifically states that the church will be taken out *beforehand*, however they do allude to it. Many Theologians have studied the scriptures to back up this theory. Namely in 2 Thessalonians chapter 2 verse 6-7, Paul says that there is a restrainer who is stopping the Antichrist being revealed and once he is removed then the Antichrist will become the world ruler. The belief is that this restrainer is the Holy Spirit and therefore the removal of the Holy Spirit will also mean the removal… or rapture of the church." He paused and went on to say, "It is in the character of God to deliver His own from the greatest times of trial. You take for example, Lot, Rahab, Israel, Noah, etc. Romans 5:9 says, 'Since we have now been justified by His blood, how much more shall we be saved from God's wrath through Him' and 1 Thessalonians 1: 10 'and to wait for His Son from heaven, whom He raised from the dead—Jesus, who rescues us from the coming wrath'."

"Well there are lots to back it up, it just doesn't stand out. I'll have to study these further," Jack said as he busily scribbled the scriptures down on his notepad.

"I'll drop over some books you might like to read. It's a fiction series about the rapture occurring and what happens to the people left here on earth. They are pretty much aligned with what we have been taught."

"They sound great, thanks."

"This should get Jack researching things," said Gabe.

"Yes." Seth replied. "We need to speak into Jack's heart and mind and let him know what the reality of all of this is. Let's keep our eyes open to counteract the enemy. They won't be happy when Jack finds out what really is going on."

Yes, lives are at stake here so we have to be vigilant."

"You called to see me Master?" Crystalyn said bowing low and squirming uncomfortably amongst the hordes of other demons gathered in front of a colossal beast sitting on a large ornate throne. The creature's eyes emanated pure evil and hatred; his teeth were like long thin spikes ready to impale their prey. His wolf like muzzle sneered at the demons standing before him. His horns were gnarled and thick, sweeping backward across his skull. His body covered in scars from great battles, both with angelic hosts but also with his own kind. He was a force to be reckoned with, a malicious being that every demon in the region feared. He was Major General Lothar, the commander of the regions army.

"What is your progress?" Lothar asked.

"I have the girl and it is only a matter of time Master, everything is going to plan," Crystalyn responded meekly.

"What form have you become this time?"

"I have befriended her as an Egyptian princess my Lord." He smiled and bowed low again.

"Good," Lothar grinned, very pleased with Crystalyn's response. "Now what is this I hear of Jack Daley?"

"I know nothing of Jack Daley, sir!" Crystalyn replied, looking around nervously in case it was something he was actually *supposed* to know.

OOOOMPH!, a tiny demon with rodent teeth landed in a crumpled heap, wincing before Lothar. Snickers were heard from the hordes from where he was pushed. Shaking with fear, he stood up to address the General. "Jack Daley will not be a problem," the small ugly frame wheezed out, "he is just curious and will not interfere with our plans."

"LIES!" Lothar roared, his voice vibrating and shaking the cold stone walls sending the dark crowded room shuffling backward in fear. "You know nothing of the saints you imbecile," he bellowed. "Curiosity is never peaked without a reason; the enemy has been working. Don't be so lax and get out there and do your job." He grabbed the small gangly demon tightly around the neck slowly squeezing him until his red bulging eyes were frantic and threw him back into the horde with a thud. Demons went tumbling, screaming, and fluttering around in a panic. Chaos and fear had erupted in the rooms of the abandoned pump station.

That night, Jack was sleeping so peacefully, until it stealthy entered the room. It slowly crept up and started baring its full weight down upon Jack's body, willing him to die, crushing the air out of him slowly but intentionally.

Jack gasped and started trying to fight back in confusion, half-dreaming and half-conscious he struggled to understand what was going on, *was this a nightmare?* he thought. He could feel his assailant smothering him but couldn't move. His eyes shut but dancing rapidly he felt paralysed, his limbs would not respond. He tried calling out, but couldn't speak, its weight was intense and meaningful. He felt the fear, but he could not wake up. He knew he was in the realm of lucid dreaming but could not break out of it. The fear was intense; he could feel it but had no power to overcome it.

It continued to crush and smother its victim mercilessly. It grinned with pleasure seeing the desperation and terror etched all over Jack's face. Its talons sank in deep and curled around Jack's larynx, its other slimy six arms wrapped tightly around his body like a boa constrictor's vice like grip.

J-J-Jesus, Jack tried hard to whisper, but nothing came of it. He couldn't speak, he couldn't move but he felt every ounce of the evil force bearing down on his chest.

Wake up, wake up. Jack willed himself to consciousness but did not succeed. *Wake up!* He felt powerless, caught in the twilight zone. He was trapped in this halogenic state of terror that was colliding with the natural plain. The entity pushed down, squeezing tight, gripping harder and harder.

"What are you up to Jack?" Its deathly voice rasped with hate and curiosity.

Jack's heart raced in terror as he heard those words project directly into his mind, he couldn't speak he was mute, and it was all over him, upon him and in him. Its black limbs clasping, locked through his torso, he could see it all in his dream like state with his eyes closed, his fear escalated. He squeaked out a sound, but it gripped harder.

Help me, help me...Jesus, Jack thought but the words could not pass through his lips. He started gasping and choking he could feel his heart racing and hear its loud echoing, the blood pounding in his ears.

"What are you looking for Jack?" it asked again, releasing its grip around his throat just enough for an answer."

His fear intensified, he still couldn't speak, he couldn't move, he couldn't breathe, he tried, and tried and tried... until he finally broke through, "JESUS!" he yelled.

"Stop pursuing this," it screamed into his conscience, as it dropped its grasp and quickly glided back though the wall into the black night.

Jack instantly became wide-awake. He saw the dark shadow silently leaving.

Seth and Gabe urgently entered the room with their swords drawn to find Jack gasping and holding his throat.

"What's wrong?" Jenny stirred sleepily, "I thought I heard you yell something."

"Sorry, I didn't mean to wake you, it's nothing sweetie... just a bad dream," Jack responded, but he knew it wasn't. He lay awake for hours thinking of what had just happened.

CHAPTER TWELVE

It was 2 am. Crystalyn spoke deep into Lora's mind, whilst Rebellion looked on in awe at the mastery at hand.

"I like how you do this," Rebellion stated with eagerness. "So, what are we doing with her tonight?" he asked.

"As always," Crystalyn spoke confidently and authoritative as if speaking to his protégé, "we go very slowly so not to spark any scepticism or confusion. We don't want to frighten her away but reel her in so she trusts completely, it's all about timing." He grinned showing his row of thin sharp teeth.

Lora was dreaming deeply. She and her princess friend Crystalyn were sitting beside the shimmering clear pool talking.

"So, is Jesus real then?" Lora asked.

"Yes, he is a highly ascended master who came to show us the path to a higher consciousness. He came to teach us how to redeem ourselves by discovering the kingdom of God within us."

"But he's God's Son right, like my dad tells the congregation?"

"Well, yes and no, you see that's a fabrication that the world has been led to believe. We are actually all gods ourselves; there is not one god but many, many gods. We all aspire to gain elevation into a higher natural state. Besides, don't believe that nonsense, how can there be just *one* when we are *all* gods?" Crystalyn emphasised.

"I thought that's how it was; I mean that's all I've grown up knowing, that's all I've been taught," Lora responded confused.

"Well you've been misled Lora, you need to think for yourself now." Crystalyn sighed sympathetically, "I really feel for the poor souls who have been indoctrinated with these kinds of lies. They are chained and bound and cannot be free until they know the real truth," Crystalyn said passionately and convincingly.

"Wow, I would never have known," Lora said stunned but admiring her friend's deep knowledge.

Rebellion smiled at Crystalyn in wonder. "You're so smooth," he praised.

"I know, but they make it so easy. They will believe *absolutely anything,*" he chuckled.

"Hi Pete it's Jack, when you get this message, well that's if you have some time, can you please call me. I have some questions. Oh, and I hope you're having a great time at your son's place too, enjoy your new grandkid. See you later."

Jack hung up the phone and went about his day still disturbed at what happened the other night. He desperately wanted to talk to Peter about it but didn't want to spoil his family holiday.

"You should see him work Master, it's amazing at what can be achieved in one night," Rebellion praised as he and Crystalyn both stood in front of Lothar.

"So Crystalyn, obviously you're making progress with the girl?"

"Yes, my sire, she is coming along nicely. I have now seeded doubt in her mind regarding her beliefs and will now attempt to distance her from her friends and family. She will trust only me for advice my Lord."

"Good, good." Lothar grinned, liking what he was hearing. "The plan seems to be coming along nicely then." He stated as his immense gaze looked over his gaggling hoard. "Has Jack Daley's enthusiasm been quashed?"

A small messenger meekly stepped forward. "Sir," it bowed low, "we are making every attempt to dissuade him from doing any further research on the subject. We have now made two attempts, but have to time it when the Guardians are not watching."

"Well… try harder, I'm hearing that he still has his nose in *that* book," he spat with venom. "And that the hosts are eagerly encouraging him to do so."

"We have everything under control sir, it will be fine."

"IT WONT *BE* FINE," Lothar yelled as he smashed his fist down and picked up his sword and swung it furiously, cracking it hard on the stone floor. The hoard scampered and scrambled backwards in fear of retribution. "You obviously do not understand you imbecile, something is up and I want to know what it is and why. Do you HEAR ME?" Lothar's voice vibrated shaking the cold stone walls, his rank breath rushing out like a gale-force wind making the messenger teeter backwards. "It's important to us because it's IMPORTANT TO THEM…GET IT?"

"Y-Y-Yes S-sir," the timid messenger stuttered in fear.

"GO NOW."

The messenger didn't waste any time getting out of his presence, he flew out and landed in a distant tree trembling before he could compose himself and fly further onward to Evensmore to deliver his dispatch.

It was 2.30 am. Again, Lora was deeply dreaming, sitting with Crystalyn under a tree on a hill in a lush grass-filled field. She could feel the wind gently caressing her cheeks.

"The fortune teller at the fair, you know…Carla, how did she know so much about me?" Lora asked.

"We all know everything about everyone, it's the universal mind. It's all knowing and all powerful. Carla has the special gift of being able to tap into it and gain the information that she needs."

"Wow, I wish I could do that."

"You can learn, I can teach you. You can also command the universe too; its power can give you the desires of your heart," Crystalyn responded happily with beautiful translucent green eyes glistening.

"I'd love that," Lora stated excitedly.

Rebellion sat and listened intently, learning the ways of Crystalyn, the familiar spirit, demon of disguise. He waited until Crystalyn had finished his nights work before he spoke.

"I think I could start doing that."

"Just like I showed you; it's easy just do it slowly and build trust."

"The spiel about the fortune teller, that was gold," Rebellion sniggered with excitement.

"I know, I love telling them that it's a *special gift*. Stupid fools," Crystalyn scoffed, extremely happy with his night's efforts.

Jack left the house and went for a walk out onto his property; he hadn't spoken to Jenny about what had been happening, as he didn't want to scare her. He needed to speak with Peter. He tried Peter's mobile phone again and sighed in dismay when it went straight to the message service.

"Hi Pete it's Jack again, listen I *really* need to talk with you. I can't explain over the phone but some weird stuff has been happening…and well…I don't know what to do. Please call me when you get a chance. I'll talk to you soon." He sighed, "Hopefully!" Jack said after he ended the call.

"Jack I'm worried about you," Jenny said as he entered the house, "you look terrible."

"I've just been having trouble sleeping, it's nothing to worry about."

"What is it? Work?"

"It's a combination of things, I'll be okay, I just need to get back into my sleeping pattern again. Don't worry," he said as he hugged her and kissed her forehead. "Now, how about a coffee?"

It was Saturday night and Meg was sleeping over at Lora's house, they did this once a month and alternated between each other's houses. As usual, they had stayed up very late into the early hours of the morning and had both fallen asleep exhausted after watching a movie marathon.

Lora was fitfully dreaming and making funny noises. It woke Meg up. She looked over at her friend and her skin started to prickle as she felt her hair stand on end. She was being watched, something malevolent was staring back at her. She couldn't make it out but she felt its eyes boring into her soul and it was not welcoming. It gave her deep shivers so she quickly snuggled back under the covers in fear and pulled the blanket over her head hoping that it would provide protection. She was terrified; the feeling was so strong it freaked her out and she lay awake for the rest of the night not game to move an inch.

Jack also was laying in fear, unable to sleep, waiting again for the assailant, but to his relief it didn't come this night.

Morning came around quickly and Jack threw himself into his work. He hadn't picked up the bible since the first night of the encounter, and was in trepidation from the warning that he received.

Seth spoke. "He needs to learn how to handle this."

"He is still new and he doesn't understand yet. He hasn't been taught, however this *will* strengthen him." Gabe responded.

"Agree… Peter will be home soon and will help him understand. In the meantime, we will be on the lookout."

"Did you find out anything?" Lothar's deep menacing voice rasped.

The meagre messenger again stood timidly, shaking before the grand beast. "The nocturnal spirit hasn't yet succeeded in its mission," it said meekly, "but I'm sure it will very, very soon," the messenger exclaimed."

"It better, else you both will no longer be living in this realm," Lothar sneered, growing impatient. "I have also been notified that Jophiel is in the region."

"It still should be fine Master, don't worry we have it under control." It squeaked timidly.

"Do you even understand who I speak of small spirit?" Lothar challenged, his fists clenched tightly with anger. "Jophiel is only sent when there is a vital mission to accomplish. SO, DON'T YOU DARE tell me that it's under control when I know what *this* host of heaven can do to us. DO YOU UNDERSTAND?" He roared with tornado like breath rushing though his fierce jowls. "FIND OUT NOW." He screamed as he smashed his giant curved sword down sending sparks across the room.

The messenger quickly left the building and flew straight away to deliver its report.

"You must make progress," it squeaked at the nocturnal spirit that was hiding in a blackness of a dark cavern in the daylight hours. "Lothar is very, *very* angry with us, you need to find out what's going on."

"Hey Lora, were you having a bad dream the other night when I stayed over?" Meg asked.

"Umm, I can't remember, No, I don't think so. I was just meeting up with Crystalyn again like I do every night."

"Oh okay."

"Why do you ask?"

"No reason, you were just making funny noises, I thought you were having a nightmare that's all."

"No, I sleep really well every night and dream so clearly." She beamed.

"Really?"

"Yeah, why do you sound so surprised?"

"Well, do you feel something watching you at night?" Meg shifted uncomfortably.

"No, do you?"

"Umm, maybe it was just my imagination then; I thought I felt something else in the room the other night, that's all."

"I've never felt it and I'm sure if there was something weird Crystalyn would tell me."

"Okay sure. Let's go get a milk shake," Meg responded quickly to change the subject and headed off in the direction of Betty's Café.

"We must rid ourselves of her, she could jeopardise everything." Crystalyn looked over at Rebellion very concerned.

"How can she jeopardise anything, she's just a stupid girl."

"Don't ever underestimate the humans' bond numskull," he spat venomously. "I've had many failures due to a nosey friendship getting in the way. She sensed me the other night, she was looking right at me… so just shut up and do as I say if you want to continue to learn this craft," he said with hatred. "Besides, if we stuff this up we will be no longer if Lothar gets a hold of us. Now get to work," he ordered.

CHAPTER THIRTEEN

Jack had lain awake in the night hours until his eyes finally succumbed to the drowsiness.

Gabe saw him first and chased the scrawny black demon down the stairs into Jack's office. Seth was close behind in hot pursuit.

It was 2.37 am when it attacked. This time it wanted an answer and Jack could feel in his dreaming state the hatred and determination emanating from it. The entity wound its several limbs around Jack's body and again squeezed his larynx tight. This time he could feel its long talons biting into him, boring into his very soul. The pressure was intense, stronger than the other times but again he felt paralysed, unable to move a muscle, his voice constricted. He felt as though he was again choking, trying to scream out.

"What are you after Jack, what are you looking for in the book?" it probed, projecting its voice into Jack's mind.

Seth and Gabe danced around the desk, the tiny demon just keeping out of harm's way, dodging, flitting and fluttering around the room its small wings beating rapidly to avoid contact. They were trying to swat it with their mighty swords.

Jack again was struck with fear, but also confused about the question, he started to panic. The massive entity squeezed him harder, he felt as though he was going to explode under the sheer pressure.

Wake up, wake up Jack c'mon wake up. Again, he willed himself to regain a conscious state. He saw the spirit its blackness enveloped him, hovered over him and thoroughly encased him. He was smothering under the heaviness of it resting upon his chest. The fear in him rose to new heights, he tried again to scream but there was nothing. It had a grip on his larynx and he could do nothing. *Please Jesus, Jesus, Jesus.* He repeated over and over loudly in his mind, willing the words to come out of his mouth. Caught between the two realms, he couldn't escape.

It danced it flitted and leered at them. But Seth and Gabe just couldn't grasp a hold of it. It was always just out of their reach.

The large entity grew impatient. "I need to know what you're looking for, why are you so consumed with Revelation?" Its rasping voice reverberated loudly throughout Jack's thoughts.

Jack squirmed, he tried to open his eyes, he yearned, pushed, and tried to make himself wide-awake, he had to fight this thing, and this had to stop. His life and his sanity depended on it; suddenly he broke through just enough to make a loud muffled cry.

Gabe heard it first and flew with all his force upwards towards Jack's room. Seth followed and both of them ploughed through the floorboards and slammed hard into the dark being, knocking it off Jack and tumbling onto the floor. Its several arms grabbled, scratching and clawing as Seth held it down, his sword to its throat ready to slice.

Jack gasped and came out of his hallucinogenic state. He got straight up, ran down the stairs, and fell on his knees and wept, shaking with fear, the sweat was pouring off him.

Jenny was still upstairs peacefully sleeping.

"What are you doing here?" Gabe demanded of the captive entity. "Why have you come?"

"I should be the one asking *you* that," it spat. "Why are such high-ranking angels guarding this mortal? Why is *he* so important?" it hissed. "One might think there is more to his destiny than we know?" It smirked.

Gabe and Seth both looked at each other. Seth spoke as he pushed his sword deeper into its skin slowly cutting its putrid epidermis. "Tell us what you are after?"

"My Master is simply curious to why Jack is so consumed in reading the book."

"He's simply curious, just like any *other* saint who wants to read our Lord's word," Gabe responded sternly.

The demon squirmed uncomfortably, at that thought. "But it's *not* just like anyone else is it? Why would two lieutenants from *Jophiel's* regiment be guarding this man, unusual don't you think?" It leered knowingly. "Obviously it *is* something isn't it?" It grinned maliciously. "You *are* up to something... I wouldn't be messing with *my* Master's plans if I were you. I've seen many members of your pathetic army slain by him."

"Shut it," Gabe said impatiently. "If you have nothing more to say then we will finish you and your silly little messenger spirit."

"He'd be long gone by now," it chuckled. "You will never win this.

You should quit now and simply give up. You are all doomed," it ranted in a frenzy of hatred whilst Seth held it down tight. "We will win, we will get far more souls than you, you just wait and see, you just *wait* and se—"

Seth cut it off as he plunged the alighted sword through the assailant. He was finished.

"Jack, I got home late last night are you alright?" Peter said over the phone.

"Pete, I need to talk to you straight away."

"Okay, I'll see you at Betty's in 20 minutes."

Meg's mother Patty was serving up scrambled eggs on toast for breakfast. "What's happening at school today?"

"We've got the sporting event on; I'm aiming to beat Lora this time." She grinned.

"Good for you… you are a fast runner."

"Yeah but Lora is faster though." She giggled.

"How is she anyway?"

"It is weird mum, she's dreaming of this friend all the time, and it's making me feel uneasy."

"They are just dreams honey, it's all harmless."

"I guess you're right, they're just dreams," she sighed. "Anyway, I had better go, we are going to jog to school together to warm up. Wish me luck." She beamed.

Jack told Peter everything, his emotions flooded his sentences, and he could hardly contain himself.

"I'm so sorry Jack I wish I got your messages sooner. Tyler, the little rascal," he chuckled, "threw my phone into the pool. I simply didn't bother getting a new one or even thought to check my message service."

"Well, it's been terrible, I don't know what to do, I can't sleep, and I don't know when it's going to happen again."

"Mmm it's strange, I have heard of this but never experienced it myself. It's obviously wanting something, or trying to stop you doing something." He pondered on this. "You said it spoke?"

"Yes, it asked me why I was consumed with reading Revelation."

"That's interesting, keep digging Jack, it's trying to stop you from finding something."

"But what? What do I have, or what am I doing? I'm really frightened Pete, I'm frightened to go to sleep, for my family…for me. I mean, I thought I was going to die the other night. It's so crazy, I don't even believe in this stuff."

"Do you believe that the bible is God's word?"

"Yes," he sighed, frustrated.

"Well, you can't believe in some of the bible and not the other, it doesn't work like that! How can you *not* believe in the demonic? Jesus cast demons out of people, he also commanded his disciples to do the same. The bible says that we do not war against flesh and blood but the spiritual realm."

"I guess… I've just not really thought about it. It certainly wasn't taught in our church back in the city. I'm not big on fiction and that's what it seems like, just fairy tales about ghosts and goblins. Besides…I'm so exhausted and feel really angry that this is all happening," Jack sighed and continued, "and I don't know what to think. I just know what I'm experiencing feels so real."

"Well, Jack I'm telling you now, it's real. There are angels and demons and there is a battle waging. Don't be so blind to go through life as a Christian thinking that this isn't true. Jack, *WE* live in the fantasy world, we are blinded to the spiritual realm, but it is there. It's the real world and you're getting a glimpse of it." He paused. "We need to pray for your protection and bind up the enemy, they do not want you to find something. I just don't know what it is yet."

"Me neither, I'm simply reading the bible for goodness sakes."

Lothar was angry, very angry. "Banished, BANISHED? Another one of *mine* gone!" he ranted, the small messenger quivered at his response.

"Keep trying to dissuade him, use what you can," he said defeated in disgust as he walked out of the dark cold room.

Jack was alone in the house, he decided to open his bible for the first time in weeks.

"Good." Seth said, "we need to keep encouraging him to seek the truth. The plan depends on it."

Gabe watched over Jacks shoulder as he skimmed through the bible pages listlessly, a little despondent and lost. Gabe reached forward and with a quick flick of his finger, flipped the pages open to Revelation.

Jack started to read.

C H A P T E R   F O U R T E E N

Crystalyn hovered over Lora in her dreams, beckoning her to go into a deeper subconscious state. His princess form took her to the blue pond again and they sat peacefully dipping their feet at the cool water's edge.

"What is my purpose?" Lora asked earnestly.

"Your purpose is to help others and to assist me in creating peace and unity in this township."

Crystalyn continued to speak into Lora's mind and she believed every word.

There was no visible moon; the clouds were thick and blanked out any speck of light that attempted to peek through from the night sky. The demons loved it, this atmosphere was exactly what they savoured.

Jack was restless; he tossed, turned, and tried to ignore the slight lump in the mattress. He laid wide-awake, waiting for sleep to overtake him and when it finally did, it had only felt like moments. He awoke with a start, jerking upright. He had heard something downstairs.

He checked Jenny; she was still sleeping peacefully, as he gently pulled back the bedcovers and stood quietly, unmoving, not breathing, but intently listening.

He heard it again.

Someone was in the house, he knew it, he felt his skin prickle and the sudden rush of adrenaline pulse through his system. He could hear his heart rate thumping inside his head as he slowly crept out the bedroom door. He walked cautiously towards the kid's rooms and peered through each of their doors to ensure they were safely sleeping. Before leaving Matthews room, he quietly reached around and grabbed the baseball bat that sat just behind the door. He slowly descended the stairs, armed and ready.

He heard the sound again, but this time something fell onto the floor making a loud clattering sound. He waited with the sensation of complete fear clasping his chest; he raised his bat ready for the swing. He would do anything to protect and defend his family.

Peter woke with a jolt; he felt a sudden pressure to pray for Jack. He quickly scrambled out of bed in obedience and fell desperately onto his knees. He started to intercede for something he didn't understand.

Jack's foot stepped off the last stair and landed on the floorboards below, it loudly creaked; he suddenly froze and took a short breath, listening and waiting, hoping that it hadn't given his position away to the intruder.

He heard the noise again.

He reached around and fumbled for the light, but as his fingers flicked the switch, the bulb brightly sparked, popped, and blew out, leaving him in complete darkness. His hair bristled... he could feel them coming towards him with a rush.

Peter continued to kneel at his bedside and pray. He didn't understand what it was about, however he could feel the sheer urgency.

Jack was hit in the chest with full force. As he staggered backwards, he swung his bat hard but connected with nothing. Suddenly he was hit from the back and shoved forcefully forward, smashing into a cupboard, rocking the contents inside. He fell onto his knees and fumbled in the darkness for his bat; he grasped it and started again to swing wildly at the blackness that surrounded him. He felt fear like never before; the atmosphere was thick and heavy with an invisible evil force. This time he could hear them... but it wasn't anything human.

Peter cried out to God, desperately interceding for whatever was happening to Jack. He prayed and prayed... and prayed.

The room was full of black demons, swooping upon Jack, taunting him, and pushing him onto the floor. One grabbed Jacks bible off the lounge chair and ripped its pages out, scattering them across the room. Another threw a lamp at Jack, hitting him hard in the shoulder.

Several jumped upon him, weighing him down. He fell hard, hitting his head on the hardwood floorboards. His head was pinned and his cheek was pressed firm, crushed on the rigid boards beneath.

"Leave it alone Jack, we *will* kill you."

He felt the hot breath against his ear.

Seth and Gabe were experiencing their own traumas, they had stayed closely to Jack, however had been separated in the fight. Jack was over the other side of the room unprotected, whilst they were staring at three enormous beings.

The largest of the three held his sword ready, its sharp steel blade was curved like a large sickle, and its jewelled handle beautifully glinted in the night obscuring its bloodied intent.

They all stared at each other, none willing to make the first move.

Peter continued to pray passionately, "God, I don't know what's happening, but protect Jack Lord. Keep him and his family from harm."

Jophiel and Chale had heard the cry, they launched into full flight, and their army's best were close behind.

Jack forced himself back onto his feet, he continued to swing violently, and he sent a glass vase smashing to the floor in his aggressive defence. He could hear the laughter from his unseen assailants. He could feel the demonic whirlwind encircling him and pressing into him. The fear rose in his throat, he did not know how to defend himself against the unseen.

Again, he felt the powerful attack from the back pushing him forcefully forward into the wall. Again, he felt the hot coarse breath against his ear. "Stop seeking and leave it alone." Its foul breath lingered in the air.

Seth made the first move, like lightening he dove down low and hard, sliding across the polished floor underneath the three massive beings trunk like legs, to arise swiftly behind them, taking them completely off guard. They didn't even have time to take a swing. Two dark beasts lurched around to defend themselves, whilst the other made his attack on Gabe. Their swords clashed and sparked. The battle was on.

Jophiel and Chale could see the small town in the far distance. They both looked at each other with concern.

"We have to make it before he is hurt...or worse." Jophiel yelled with apprehension. Their wings were flat against their backs; they were at full speed, like hot blazing comets piercing through the cold blackness before them.

Jack could feel the weight bearing down on him. He was beyond fear; the paralysing panic engulfed him like an icy liquid pulsating through his veins. He was drenched in sweat, his jaw was tight, his breathing was rapid, and his heart thudded fiercely in his chest.

"Stop reading the book." It again rasped in his ear.

Gabe was fast, and had already managed to maim his attacker; he left him lying on the floor writhing in agony from his missing leg, arm, and wing.

Seth had only one attacker left, the other was now simply a cloud of thick grey smoke swirling in the tumultuous dark evil swarm.

Gabe ran towards Jack to pick off the black hellish demons holding him down.

"Use your authority Jack." He cried.

Through his fear-ridden mind, Jack had faintly heard something.

"Do what Peter taught you," Gabe again shouted as he continued to sweep back and forth with his sword, cutting and slashing torsos and wings, smashing through the tornado of blackness.

Jack heard it clearly this time and he remembered. "In the name of Jesus," he shouted, "I command you to leave my house now."

The sudden rush of the demonic exit was like a vacuum sucking the air out in an atomic blast. As the hordes of demons were leaving the house, Chale, Jophiel and their mighty armies descended with a loud war cry echoing through the darkness. Their thundering wings resounded through the cool night air, their radiating light pierced through the darkness as they sent terror into their enemy. Not all escaped to tell of the tale.

Peter felt the urgency suddenly dissipate; he hesitated before he picked up the phone.

"Well done. You saved him." Jophiel commended Gabe and Seth, as his army continued scouting the area for more of the enemy. Some were still chasing after demons, streaking through the night sky in hot pursuit to claim victory.

"They took us completely by surprise," Gabe said, still edgy from the battle.

"We were not ready Captain." Seth commented despondently.

Jophiel reached out and put his hand on Seth's shoulder. "You did well my friend." He comforted. "Fear not for this will only strengthen him."

Jack sat on the lounge after he had finally managed to calm his nerves. He was assessing his wounds and the damage to the house when the phone rang.

"Jack, are you alright" Peter spoke desperately.

"No…well… I am now, but no… Pete, I don't know what just happened." Jack detailed emotionally. He then recounted the whole story.

"We must encourage Jack to continue," said Jophiel, addressing the angels gathered. "I'm hoping that this will spur him on towards the truth and not deter his hunger. Don't let the enemy near him from now on. We must be diligent and ensure that the plan is not hindered."

They all nodded in agreement.

Seth and Gabe made sure to guard Jack closely.

CHAPTER FIFTEEN

The leaves had turned a mixture of rusty red and yellow, most had curled on the ground, but some still hung desperately to the bare branches. The late autumn chill had set in and winter was edging around the corner. Mustard had his thick winter rug on and was lazing in his stable while the Daley's fire was gently flickering, comfortably warming the house in the morning frost. Jack had continued to spend the passing months researching the bible, his hunger for more evidence unquenched. He had not seen another attack since that night and he was relieved, he felt strong, confident, and safe.

This was a cold Thursday morning and Peter and Jack were sitting by a warm, sun-filtered window at Betty's Café.

"It's the Holy Spirit holding the Antichrist back!" Peter stated.

"No, I don't think so Peter, how do we know He's not referring to a specific angel assigned to hold back the Antichrist and when he is removed the lawless one will be revealed. I'm not seeing the evidence anywhere in the scripture, so why does it necessarily have to be the Holy Spirit, or the church?" Jack asked.

"Well, I've always believed... and been taught that."

"Taught by whom... by man?" Jack interrupted.

"Yes," he smiled as he said, "by man, that the church will be taken out then the Antichrist will appear."

"So where are they getting it from, where in scripture? Where from *God's* word?"

"Only in 2 Thessalonians 2:7, that I know of."

"So therefore the 'One' may not necessarily mean the Holy Spirit."

"Maybe, I guess I've never really questioned it because they were great scholars and Theologians. I simply believed them."

Jack raised his eyebrows. "They are still men, not God," Jack continued. "Okay if what you say is true then Jesus will have to appear *two* more times, one secretly when He comes to get the church and another when He condemns the people – that is Armageddon, is that true?"

"Mm," Peter mumbled unconvincingly.

"Look, I don't know if I'm right or wrong, but I do know that God has put this desire in me to find out the truth about this. I feel He keeps telling me not to listen to man's theory on this, but only to His voice. It seems that every day something else points to us having to endure this whole tribulation thing. But... I also feel like I know nothing, I'm not a scholar, I didn't go to bible school so who am I to question this teaching? You know what... I really hope I'm wrong because I don't want my family or myself to have to go through this, I want the easy way out too." Jack paused. "But what if I'm not wrong Peter? What then, how will it affect the church? You know that scripture that says that many will be offended and fall away?"

"Yes."

"Well, what if Jesus is talking about this very thing?"

"How do you mean?"

"So how will it affect the Christians who think we don't have to endure, who are banking on going up to Heaven beforehand?" He paused. "Like Shaun for example? Do you think that they will be upset that they *have* to endure this and get angry with God for letting us go through this? Maybe become offended and maybe even fall away?"

"Mm you could be on to something here - go on."

"I guess what I'm saying is this. If you were living your life happily and then found out that tomorrow you would have to fight the heavy weight boxing champion of the world how would you feel... or fare in the fight?"

"I'd be really upset, scared and would probably get pulverised in the first round."

"My thoughts exactly. But what if you knew beforehand, like say two or three years?"

"Well, I'd have more of a chance because I would prepare, train, and get in shape and at least give my best fight... even at my age," Peter chuckled.

"Exactly if people aren't prepared they will be susceptible to caving in, to cracking under the pressure, to not stand and fight for what they believe in."

"So what are you getting at, that we are not prepared? I have always said to the people to be prepared for the return of Christ, I've never told them otherwise."

"But what if that *return* is at the very end, not at the beginning? I'm saying that we need to get a strong message across to prepare for the end times and not think we are leaving beforehand. How serious has your messages been?"

"Ah... I guess, I tell them but I'm not sure that they take it too seriously. I mean I haven't preached on the end times because I've always believed that we would be taken up before the tribulation occurred."

"Well, I believe that the message needs to be stronger, to explain not to hang onto the hope that we are going up before this happens but to live as though we have to go through this otherwise we don't stand a chance. From reading into the scriptures, many will suffer under torture, cave in, accept the mark, and worship the beast. Numerous Christians will end up going to Hell because they were not strong enough in their faith. They fell and lost it in the end."

"Wow, God really has been working on you!" Peter shook his head in amazement at seeing Jack's passion.

Jack became even more passionate. "We have to have an attitude, a mindset as though we will go through this tribulation. We need to be fervent in pursing God *right now* Peter, to immerse ourselves in knowing and learning His word, get closer to Him and strengthen our faith. If we do this, we will endure it and not be deceived. If I'm wrong and we go out beforehand then that's *fantastic*, we haven't lost anything but gained a greater relationship with Christ and believe me, I'm all for that scenario."

"Me too."

Gabe and Seth clapped their hands and smiled.

"I don't believe in God anymore," Lora said to Meg as they were casually having their lunch, sitting with their backs against an old tree in the school grounds.

"What?" Meg replied in astonishment.

"Well, Crystalyn says that there are many Gods, many religions and all of them lead to utopia, one universe, it's really *one* religion, Heaven or whatever you want to call it. It doesn't matter it's all the same. Crystalyn's been teaching me how to control the energy of my mind and body and once I've done that then I can advance to conquering the energy of the sun, moon, earth, and the greater universe. I then will have a full understanding of truth and creation and myself. So therefore, there isn't a God…we are all gods in ourselves, the power is *within* us." She finished with her hand on her chest for emphasis.

"WOW!" Meg looked at Lora in astonishment. "I've never heard you talk like this. What about your father… he's going to absolutely flip."

"Well that's just it… who would want to follow a God like *HE* believes in, all these rules and regulations. Do this, don't do that. I'm sick of it and my mum just puts up with being trampled on like a doormat. She does everything, yes sir, no sir, your preaching was wonderful, blah, blah, blah," Lora said mockingly. "It's sickening. I don't want to follow a God who expects you to act like that; I want freedom Meg that's what I want, the freedom to be me. Crystalyn seems so happy to have *that* freedom, and with being in another realm, that's how we can meet in the universal conscience."

"Mm you're really getting into this aren't you? I mean come on Lora, it's not *real*, it's just make-believe. You can't take this seriously surely!"

"It's not fantasy!" Lora snapped, her anger showing. "You can't say that, Crystalyn *is* real, and a very good friend to me. Haven't you been listening to what I just told you?"

"WHOA Lora, settle. Don't be so serious," Meg replied trying to calm her down. "Lora you've *REALLY* changed. I don't think meeting Crystalyn has been very good for you. In fact… I think it's been the worst thing that's happened to you…you've just changed so much."

"You're *SO* wrong Meg. Meeting Crystalyn has been the *BEST* thing that ever happened to me. You obviously don't know me well enough to see how I've been so much happier."

"Ah sorry, but all I see is you are more confused frustrated and angry at the world… not happier," Meg said sarcastically.

"Take me as I am Meg, cause this is the new me, I'm just standing up for myself, like Crystalyn is teaching me. I'm the one in control of my life and I can command the universe to give me what *I* want, not rely on anyone else. You're just jealous and you don't understand me." She paused. "So, if you don't like it then don't hang around me anymore."

Those words hit Meg with a thud; she was stunned and hurt at the same time. Confused at where this simple conversation had led. "Lora I'd like to stay friends but you're really starting to worry me. You've changed."

"Well you decide what you want to do, I don't need you, I've got Crystalyn," she snapped.

"Okay then… looks like you've made your decision. I'll see you around." With that said Meg got up, brushed off her school dress and walked away with tears streaming down her face wondering what had happened to her best friend.

Crystalyn sat quietly beside Lora and was extremely pleased.

Rebellion spoke, "Done." He grinned back at Crystalyn satisfactorily.

That night, Meg cried herself to sleep.

CHAPTER SIXTEEN

It was a glorious mid-winter's morning and the sunrays were dappling through the branches of the trees in front of Betty's Café. Betty had just opened her doors and Jack and Peter were the first to order breakfast.

"So what's happening now?" Peter asked Jack whilst sipping his cappuccino.

"Well, it's moving into production, they are asking for more volunteers to be the first to have it implanted, everything is ready. We've been tracking the previous people who volunteered for the testing for the last few months and it's working successfully. It's had great reviews and feedback from the users; they love the convenience of it."

"Wow, so soon, who would have thought," Peter said astonished.

"I don't know what to think anymore. Here I am working on a technology that can destroy thousands, but I still feel peaceful about staying on this project. Weird!"

"Not weird, God's Plan!"

"Yeah I know… I trust Him, it's just hard when my brain gets involved and tries to rule over my heart. Jen says I think too much. I can't help it that's the way I'm wired," he said to Peter with a smile. "Anyway, I've been doing more research and I'm more and more convinced that we will not be raptured before the tribulation period."

"Well you've put a pretty convincing argument together so far Jack, I've had a lot to chew on since our last catch-up."

Jack laughed. "Well you know what they say…opinions are like noses, everyone's got one and they all come with holes in them."

Peter laughed. "Ah yes, how true, I like your humility." He smiled.

Jack continued on a serious note. "I just feel like God is just leading me to evidence pointing to endurance. I've been thinking about the world situation at the moment, you know with the economic crisis, the wars and terrorism, it's really interesting to see that nearly every country is struggling and has gone into enormous debt for survival."

"Yes, I know what you're saying. This scenario reminds me of the bible story of Joseph."

"What, his multi-coloured coat?" Jack smiled and chuckled.

"No," Peter smiled and said, "you see, Joseph was commissioned to save Egypt. He took a 5th of all produce from the people in the land for seven years whilst there was plenty. When the famine hit the people came to him for food and he sold them back the produce. When the people could no longer give him money for the produce, he asked for their livestock. Now, you have to realise that livestock back then meant that they had a way of living, that is, cows bring milk, sheep for clothing and meat, horses for travel, chickens for food. So when the livestock was gone, it produced even more poverty in the land, as the people could no longer even be self-sufficient. When the people could no longer give Joseph their livestock they told him that they would give themselves and their land to the Pharaoh in exchange for food, this was fine because all Joseph wanted was to save the people. So when the famine was close to the end, Joseph told the people to go back to the land, which was now all owned by Pharaoh, and sow the seed that they had been given. However, one fifth of their produce belonged to the Pharaoh. So in essence, the people were working for the government on government land. So, do you see how desperation can lead to government dominion and control?"

"But we are not in famine," Jack replied.

"No, but we are in a similar situation where our country can be brought to its knees. People are desperate now. We are very reliant on the economy and if it gets any worse, people will be looking for a way out. Look at the Great Depression it started with the fall in stock prices in 1929 and created worldwide fear and devastation. This type of scenario leads to the perfect time for governments to step in and have the people's total reliance on them."

Jack pondered for a second before he spoke. "Well, maybe this is what it's all about. This is how the mark will be implemented. The world will be in a position that its people are so desperate and reliant on the government that they will gladly take the mark."

"Exactly, but I'm still hoping that we will be removed from this world before it gets to that point."

"I know and so do I, but I'm not totally convinced. As I was mentioning before, I feel that God's people will have to endure."

"Useless idiots, how hard is it to stop a mere human?" Lothar fumed.

"He's heavily guarded, they won't leave his side," a tiny meek voice returned. "Besides, he doesn't have any evidence, does he? It's simply his theory with nothing to back it up, our scheme is engrained throughout the world, it can't be changed easily without solid proof. The Christians believe it as truth my Lord." It assured shakily, not knowing how Lothar would respond to his sudden boldness.

"Mmm... yes maybe you're right." He paused and tapped his long black talon on his gargantuan chin. "That preacher will take some convincing anyway. This town is engrained with the teaching so maybe it won't matter, he may simply be harmless to our cause." He thought about it further and said, "But still be on guard, I don't like the way he is being protected by such high-ranking hosts, it may come to nothing, but if I know my enemy," he paused in deep thought, "they are up to something. Leave me!" he signalled with his giant clawed hand.

The messenger flew out of the window quickly relieved to survive another day.

CHAPTER SEVENTEEN

Three weeks later

"That was such a lovely dinner Jenny, thank you so much for inviting me around."

"You're more than welcome Peter," she smiled as she took away the dishes and started to pack the dishwasher.

"Oh, I'll help you do those," Peter stated.

"No, just relax, why don't you and Jack go into the lounge, I'll follow later with some coffee and desert when I'm done here," she happily said.

Peter wandered into the lounge and sat opposite Jack in a large soft leather chair.

"Okay Jack. I'm prepared for you now." He grinned, eager for the debate to start again. "I too have been thinking about your argument, about us not going out before the tribulation. So I want you to consider this fact. Noah was saved from the flood, Daniel was saved from the lions, and Shadrach, Meshach, and Abednego were saved from the furnace and were untouched by fire. Our God saves His people; He takes them out of harm's way," Peter said with assurance.

"Yes, I agree… you're totally correct, and I too have thought about this. However, the common theme is that they *still* had to go through these situations. Noah had to endure the flood. He wasn't miraculously beamed up into Heaven and saved, he had to prepare and build the ark, load the animals and ride out the storm. Daniel had to go into the lion's den and those three boys had to make a stand and go into the fire. I never said that God would not be with us, but I believe like Noah, Daniel and the boys that we will have to go through this, for how long I'm not sure, but we will have to endure part... or all of it. Endurance is all through the bible, I'm not saying that we *won't* be supernaturally helped and protected, but I still believe the enemy will persecute us. I believe that those who have a strong relationship with Christ will have the strength to get through this. But that's the key, *a strong relationship*, because we will be tested. Look here," Jack said as he started reading some bible passages that he had been studying.

"Matthew 24:12-13 says that, 'Because of the increase of wickedness, the love of most will grow cold, but he who stands firm to the end will be saved.' And Daniel 7:25-26 says, 'He will speak against the Most High and oppress His holy people and try to change the set times and the laws. The holy people will be delivered into his hands for a time, times and half a time.' That's three and a half years," Jack added, "but the court will sit, and his power will be taken away and completely destroyed forever.' And Revelation 14: 10-12 '...There will be no rest day or night for those who worship the beast and its image, or for anyone who receives the mark of its name. This calls for patient endurance on the part of the people of God who keep His commands and remain faithful to Jesus.' There's so much more Peter," Jack exclaimed as he continued to read out the passages that he had book marked in his bible.

"Also, take the passage in 2 Thessalonians 2: 3 '... Don't let anyone deceive you in any way, for that day will not come until the rebellion occurs and the man of lawlessness is revealed, the man doomed to destruction.' And Matthew 24:24-31 states that, 'Immediately after the distress of those days the sun will be darkened, and the moon will not give its light; the stars will fall from the sky, and the heavenly bodies will be shaken. Then will appear the sign of the Son of Man in heaven. And then all the peoples of the earth will mourn when they see the Son of Man coming on the clouds of Heaven, with power and great glory. And He will send his angels with a loud trumpet call, and they will gather His elect from the four winds, from one end of the heavens to the other'."

Jack paused, checking that Peter was still with him. "This passage specifically says that after these things happen that *all* nations will see Jesus return and they will mourn at the realisation that He is King and *then* we will be gathered up. There are many more scriptures, but I won't go on. However, what really got me was this sentence in John '...and I will raise him up at the last day'. It's repeated four times in chapter 6. So it got me thinking, what is the last day? There are many references to the Lord's Day, that it is a day of His return and the destruction of all sinners. So is Matthew 24:24-31 referring to the last day? I think it is and this will be the time when we go heavenward and not beforehand," Jack concluded.

"WOW!" Peter nodded his head in agreement. "You know, I cannot believe how much you've changed over the last 14 months that we've known each other. God is really stirring your heart on this. Okay, what about Matthew 24:40-42 where it states that, 'Two men will be in the field; one will be taken and the other left. Two women will be grinding with a hand mill; one will be taken and the other left. Therefore keep watch, because you do not know on what day your Lord will come?' Peter paused before he continued. "This is talking about the day Jesus whisks His believers away in the rapture, this is what the Theologians state as proof for this occurrence happening in the future, and I believe it to be so."

"Yes, I definitely can see how it can be derived as such. However, I too have pondered this scripture, and I feel that it needs to be taken in the full context of the passage, not just the end sentence. When you read the full passage, Jesus is talking about the days of Noah being like the coming of the Son of Man. He's talking about the evil in the world and these sentences, I feel, are simply referring to one of the righteous being saved, like when they boarded the ark, and the other is the evil person being left behind to perish in the flood. I don't feel that this supports a secret rapture occurring before the tribulation at all; it's just simply stating that the righteous will be taken and that could be on the very last day when Jesus returns."

Peter interjected before Jack could continue. "Well what about the passage in Revelation 3:10-11. 'Since you have kept my command to endure patiently, I will also keep you from the hour of trial that is going to come on the whole world to test the inhabitants of the earth. I am coming soon. Hold on to what you have, so that no one will take your crown.' Now this is solid evidence that Jesus will not let us suffer and will return for us quickly before the hour and this is what we were taught at bible school by top scholars."

Jack earnestly responded. "Yes, again, I'm not refuting what you're saying, however, do you think that Jesus is actually telling us that He will *always* be with us until the very end and that He will help us through this hour of testing. That He will be with us to help us avoid temptation, just like when He was praying in John 17:15 and said, 'My prayer is not that you take them out of the world but that you protect them from the evil one.'"

Jack paused before continuing, "Pete, I can see your view and how you are reading it this way but I simply see it differently as I don't believe that He's saying that we are departing but simply stating that we will have much help in this hour. Also think about this… what if the hour of trial that He is talking about is actually Armageddon? What if the Last Day is the hour of trial, which is actually the great battle and He will take us out *just* before it starts?"

"Okay," Peter sighed, putting his hands in the air and feeling a little conquered, "you make several good points that I simply cannot argue. I've been praying about this too, every time we meet you are stirring my spirit and making me see it differently and it's going against all I've been taught… but I think I'm starting to believe that you are right. As much as I don't want to say it and wish you were wrong, my spirit confirms it. I too have been struggling with your concept, as I really don't want to believe that what you're saying is truth, I just don't know how to process it. I've been asking God to break down my own barriers and belief system, because all the teachings I've heard on this subject have been about taking the church out before the tribulation. Not one bible teacher, lecturer, preacher or Theologian that I've come across, has said that we weren't leaving before the suffering started. It's been engrained into the system as truth and from what you're saying it seems as though it's all been false doctrine…a huge *lie* to deceive us." Peter paused. "And sadly, and unbeknown to me, I guess I felt a security, a strange safety in thinking that we will be saved. So, I am coming around Jack." Peter smiled. "God has been working on me, it's hard to swallow that I possibly have been teaching God's people incorrectly, that I too have been deceived in thinking that we will be saved in the way that *we* want to be saved." Peter sighed with a slight curl of his mouth.

"So how do you feel now? I mean, I could be totally wrong," Jack stated.

"No Jack, I think you're right. As I said I have been praying and slowly coming around, I just wanted to put forward some more arguments before I gave in to you." He winked cheekily as he continued. "But to be honest I'm feeling very nervous actually. I'm concerned for God's people and myself. I mean it puts a different spin on things now doesn't it. We can't just say, 'Oh well we won't have to go through it, lucky us, poor them.' It's a bit overwhelming and I have a sense of urgency to get people right with God. Get them prepared by increasing their faith and relationship with God."

Peter paused. "That's the only thing that will get us through. I feel that I now need to set things straight in the church and to reveal what God has shown you and to ask for forgiveness for my own shortcomings in this matter. I should have studied this myself instead of blindly following others before me. It shows that we must put our trust in God's word, not in man's opinions, views, or claims. We must pray and listen to what God is telling us. Exactly as you have been doing Jack, I really take my hat off to you, I'm so proud of you. You have come into Christianity with no pre-conceptions, hardly knowing the bible when I first met you and God has really used this child like belief. This is why He states to come to Him like little children, because children don't come into this world with pre conceptions and existing beliefs. You can tell them that a bunny lays eggs at Easter and they believe it whole-heartedly. This is the childlike faith that Jesus was talking about. Unfortunately, we take on board people's opinions, or what they deem is a *word* from God."

"Well it says that people will be deceived," Jack said.

"Yes, and they will if they are not grounded in Christ, knowing the truth. The enemy is extremely cunning, and will use any measures to steal God's people away, even by mimicking Him. Take the verse in Matthew 24:24-25, 'For false messiahs and false prophets will appear and perform great signs and wonders to deceive, if possible, even the elect. See, I have told you ahead of time.'... You're right, it's all been a lie, and people who are not strong will fall for it and bow down. Jesus explicitly states how He will return so we must not be fooled into thinking it has changed."

"I'm glad you're now with me on this, I thought I may have been way, way off." Jack smiled with sense of relief.

"No, God is using you to get the message across that we cannot be lax in our spirituality. You know, this has greater implications than what we are talking about here. The fact that Christians are being deceived into thinking that they would not have to endure; they are also becoming nonchalant in spreading the word of God too. It's like the security of knowing that they are going up beforehand is leading them to not only be slack in their relationship with Jesus but also in telling others. As Shaun said, some are even thinking that they will have a second chance if they miss the first coming. What you said before about the restrainer not being the Holy Spirit, I now think you are right. It can't be because 1 Corinthians 12:3 says, 'Therefore I want you to know that no one who is speaking by the Spirit of God says, 'Jesus be cursed,' and no one can say, 'Jesus is Lord,' except by the Holy Spirit.' So really, if people think that they have a second chance to come to God after the rapture then it's false because a person can only come to Christ through the Holy Spirit, there is no other way. So it's definitely not the Holy Spirit who is removed."

Peter smiled shaking his head in realisation of the years that he was misled. "You're right Jack, there is *no* pre-tribulation secret rapture... it's been a huge lie all along. We have simply been tricked, and have become lazy with our own faith. I'm not speaking for all, there are a lot of people out there doing their best to spread the gospel, but it seems that many Christians have lost their fire and are happy to coast to the end. We, as the body of Christ, have lost our desire to know Him intimately, we are just happy to be born again but not grow in our relationship, but we have to otherwise we won't survive. I don't care if I die because it means to be with Christ, but I don't want to see people tricked and deceived. This is worse than death, to spend an eternity in Hell, a never-ending torture. I can't bear the thought of not having an opportunity to save someone from that suffering."

"You're right," Jack said, "the best way to immobilise your opponent is to lure them into a false sense of security and that's just what Satan has done. By spreading this belief system throughout the Christian faith, it has caused them to become stagnant and lazy. It's like country *A* telling country *B* that they will no longer attack so, in good faith, country *B* decreases their military forces, relaxes and then WHAM, country *A* attacks and gets the upper hand. Anyway, if this I-Chip is any indication of how quickly we are moving into the final days then this is really urgent."

"Yes, you're right ... you are right!"

Both Jack and Peter suddenly looked over toward the TV screen. A news topic had caught their attention, so Jack quickly unmuted the sound so they could listen.

"The economic downturn, increase of war, terrorist attacks and one world government will be the topic of the global INAT forum held here in Jerusalem." The newsreader stated on the television. "Jason Crane's speech will aim to encourage the world leaders to find a solution to these growing problems that are threatening our very existence."

"What do you think of this Jason Crane guy?" Peter asked Jack.

"Well I asked God the same thing and I got, 'A wolf in sheep's clothing.' So if God doesn't trust him, neither do I." Jack continued, "It's exactly what Ben said, our country and others around the world for that matter are in so much debt. I did some research today and, in our country alone, each newborn baby, in effect, already owes the government $70,000. I'm not sure about smaller per capita countries, but what are we doing to our next generation? People are so overwhelmed; they are looking for answers now to get them out of trouble. And they'll probably look to this guy for the answers."

"A bit like the story of Joseph don't you think?" Peter said.

Jack just smiled.

CHAPTER EIGHTEEN

The sun was shining, birds were chirping on this glorious Saturday morning. Sarah was already in the arena riding Mustard and May was instructing her. Matthew and Ben were on their motorbikes checking the cattle and horses and Jack was aimlessly wandering around the farm. He wandered into the old wooden barn and thought that he should get some hay for Mustard when Sarah had finished. The smell of fresh Lucerne hay and dust lingered, and it took some time for his eyes to adjust to the dimness inside. *They should get some windows in here he thought.* He wandered over to an old tractor and leant his back against it, facing outward towards the big barn doors, enjoying the view of his daughter happily riding around the arena in the distance.

"It's time," Seth said to Gabe.

Gabe gently lifted his majestic sword and it started to emanate a bright penetrating light. He gently laid its piercing tip against the old dusty and broken carriage as he delicately scraped it along its cracked wooden side. 'Screeeeeeeeech' the sound rang out though the barn.

Jack jumped, startled with the unusual noise. *That was weird,* he thought as he walked curiously over towards the old carriage to see where the noise had come from, thinking it may have been a rat. He laid his hand upon the damaged structure, its wood badly gouged, scratched, and splintered in some areas, clearly unrepairable. *You are a mess*, he said aloud to himself. *What happened to you eh? Must have been a pretty bad accident.* He continued to lean over and peer into and around the carriage surveying its damaged and misshapen frame.

Seth motioned to Gabe, "Now," he said.

Gabe put his sword into the carriage under the broken and collapsed passenger seat and gave it a quick shove. 'POP'.

Jack quickly wheeled around to see where the strange sound had come from. He watched as an old dinted canister rolled out from the passenger door, clunked down the smashed stair and landed on the dusty floor with a thud before his feet.

What's this? he thought, as he leant over to pick up the dusty and damaged cylinder. He held it for a while and looked it over before he tried to pry off its lid. *Mmm this isn't easy*; he thought as he struggled with it. It wasn't going to budge. Gabe decided he couldn't wait and held out his sword, touching the canister with the glowing tip.

'THOOP' the lid popped off into Jack's hand, *this is getting weirder* Jack thought. He looked inside to see some yellowed paper rolled up like an old preserved manuscript. He gently pulled it out. *It looks like a letter*, he whispered as he gently rolled out the pages and started to read...

12th day of November 1831

My dear Daniel,

Oh, where do I start? I am in utter turmoil! I will try to make sense of what has happened, therefore I am writing this so not to miss any detail for when I arrive this morning to see you and stop you from presenting our new theory at the ministry conference.

Firstly, my dear friend please let me explain. Our discovery is nothing but a lie, a deception from the enemy himself. I know this because an angel from our great Lord himself came to me last night. I will try to explain in detail what occurred.

I was asleep, weary from my long travels, when a strong wind came blustering through the window blowing the curtains and startling me. I was certain that I had closed the window due to the brisk night air but it was not any ordinary wind, for when I opened my eyes the power and the light that emanated throughout the room was near blinding. When my eyes adjusted, I saw the angel of the Lord standing at the end of my bed. I was instantly fear stricken and could not move nor speak; it was as though I was frozen. The angel spoke and said, "Do not be afraid, for I have come to deliver a message from Jehovah your God."

I could not utter, but just laid there staring wide-eyed in fear, waiting. He continued to speak.

"Benjamin, servant of the Most High God look closely at what I have come to show you."

Daniel, it was like a window opening at the end of my bed and a clear vision appeared within it, it was most extraordinary and frightening at the same time.

I looked intently at this window and watched carefully; this is the account of the horror I saw.

People, crowds of people were gathered together. It must have been hundreds of thousands or maybe even millions, I couldn't tell as the mass went beyond my vision. However, there was something wrong with these people, many were emaciated and impoverished and looked as though they were starving. As they were crying out, I watched as a powerful man stood in a temple and ordered these people to bow down to him. He said that he would give them what they need if they worship him. Some did, but others refused. Therefore, he laughed and said that the God they believed in will not come to save them. He said that he is the true and living God and they must obey his commands, and bow down and worship him. I watched as many people started to weep and become angry with our Lord. I heard them cry out in anguish, looking heavenward saying, "You lied, you said that you would come and save us before this time, what kind of God are you?" They started to blaspheme God, I watched as many turned away from their faith in anger and desperation, offended that they had not been delivered from their distress. I could hear some of them saying that this man must be God because of the signs and started to walk forward with their arms raised in worship. I started to weep as I watched so many willingly bow down to this powerful man and lose their salvation. "Why aren't they being saved?" I cried out, "Why are they angry at God?" I started to sob.

The angel once again spoke and said, "Benjamin, they are deceived. Do not deliver your message tomorrow for it is a message straight from the evil one to destroy God's people, to distort the truth and to lure them into falsehood about not having to endure to the end. It will weaken them and hinder their faith."

I observed closely, as many people walked forward to receive a mark on their skin and pledge their allegiance to this man. I heard them say that he must be the true God because their God was supposed to deliver them before this troubled time, therefore he must be their redeemer. I also saw that those who did stand firm and refuse were killed. I started to weep; this was far too much to bear;

Then, this vision suddenly disappeared and another came into view. I watched intently as I saw Jesus returning, with a flash of lightening throughout the heavens, all the kings and nations throughout the world could see him. I saw this amazing sight, too much for mere words to describe. Many of our Christian brothers and sisters rose up and met our Lord in mid-air. I watched in awe as everyone in the world could see His return. All kings fell down on their knees and mountains trembled. Then Jesus, the Lord himself looked right into my eyes, and spoke directly to me. "Benjamin, very soon I will come. Tell my people to endure, be strong, and resist temptation and do not be deceived. Blessed are those who endure until the end, they will earn the crown of life."

Then the vision vanished. The angel turned to me and spoke once again.

"Benjamin, you have been given an account of the future, take heed of what you have seen. There will always be followers who fall away, however, many more will fall away if Daniel delivers his message," he said gravely. "You must stop what has begun as it is not of the Lord."

With that Daniel, I started to cry out with overwhelming anguish for forgiveness and the angel reached out and touched me, and the love was immeasurable. He said, "Do not be upset servant of God for you are very much loved." The peace swept over me and I felt restored. I looked up at him and he said, "Go at once!"

That's when I woke up Tommy. I am writing this while he is preparing the horses as I am hastily making my way back to see you Daniel. We must not share this theory because it is not truth and will deceive many Christ followers into believing that they will not have to endure until the end. It is clear now to me the deception that the enemy has laid. Cunningly, it will make people think that they do not have to be concerned for the troubles in the end times, if we speak of our theory, many people will believe they will be taken up heavenward, and saved beforehand. It is a lie that we have been fed Daniel, and we must not share it. It must be stopped.

I eagerly wait to meet with you and tell you of this account in person, but for fear that I may miss any detail, I will have you read this letter first.

Your brother in Christ,
Father Benjamin Harvey.

Jack stood there silently in amazement, barely moving as he re-read the fragile letter again in awe. He lent back against the old carriage to steady himself, marvelling at how remarkable this old letter was, feeling thankful and overwhelmed from the message he read before him. "WOW! This is exactly what God is telling me. Thank you, Father!" he exclaimed as tears started to well up in his eyes, his heart full of overpowering relief at the confirmation that God had given him. "Thank you so much God for showing me that this is of you, that I am on the right track, Father you are so awesome." He started to just thank and praise God over and over, his heart bursting with appreciation, reverence and excitement all at once.

After several minutes, Jack composed himself, wiped the tears of relief and joy from his face, and placed the letter back into the canister... but ensuring that the lid wasn't on too tight. He heard the motorbikes pull up outside and decided to go over and show Ben what had been hidden inside the broken old carriage for so many years.

Undetected eyes were watching Jack from a dark corner of the barn. Unbeknownst to the Guardians, a scrawny little demon saw everything that had just occurred.

A screech and a ruckus erupted in the old pump station as a flutter of membranous wings from a tiny black creature landed in front of Lothar.

"I bring urgent news great Master," he panted, trying to catch his breath, a look of concern upon his ugly, misshapen, impish face. "They have found *THE* letter!"

"WHAAAT?" he said exploding with a roar, his voice vibrating from wall to wall. A mass of demons started fleeing in all directions to avoid any wrath that may come from this disturbing news.

"Why has this been found, it was supposed to be DESTROYED!"

he bellowed, his screaming voice echoing through the empty cold, dark rooms. "It should NOT EXIST!" He screamed standing and waving his sword at the little imp. "Are you sure?"

"Y-y-yes M-mm- Master," he stammered, "I saw the Guardians show Jack Daley and he read it out loud sir."

"How did THEY have it?" he fumed as he wheeled around staring angrily outwards towards his troops.

"It, well, it w-was hidden in the old c-c-carriage all along sir," the small demon replied terrified at what may happen next.

"Where is Crechus?" he hissed. "Send me Crechus!" Lothar was fuming, his hair bristling, drool cascading down his jowls, his eyes glowing red with anger. "Bring me Crechus NOW!" he screamed as his giant black sword came down, cutting one demon in half, leaving a swirl of black mist in its place. With a panic, the scrawny messenger flew terror-stricken out of a broken, jagged window in a desperate search of Crechus.

CHAPTER NINETEEN

It was Monday and Crystalyn took a deep breath and transformed into the beautiful princess Lora had come to know. Crystalyn had become so real to Lora to the point that Lora did not have to go to sleep any more for them to meet. They could have a conversation at any time and it was proving to be a distraction.

"Lora March, what did you just say?" Mrs Pempie her teacher asked in annoyance.

Lora giggled and looked directly where Crystalyn was standing, invisible to anyone else. "Nothing Mrs Pempie," she chided and tried not to make any more disturbances. "Crystalyn," she whispered, "stop it; you're going to get me into trouble."

Meg sat across the room and just rolled her eyes at the scene that was becoming more and more frequent every day. She was annoyed with Lora but at the same time very, very concerned.

Peter, the Jacksons and the Daley's were gathered together in May Jackson's kitchen.

"This is amazing Jack," Peter said, "it's like God has confirmed everything that you have been feeling." He smiled.

"I know," Jack replied, "I can hardly believe it myself, I had to re-read it several times before it sunk in. I mean, what an amazing find," he exclaimed with excitement.

"Well, who would of thought?" Ben declared, throwing his arms up with flamboyancy. "After all these years sitting in that old barn. See May," he turned towards her, "there was a reason why we Jacksons couldn't part with that old thing." He smiled. May looked back at him with a loving grin and patted him on the back with a knowing smile.

"I'm not sure what you believe in Ben, but this letter is pretty controversial," Jack stated.

"Oh Jack, I believe in what the bible says, always have. We only go to Reverend March's church because of tradition. I know he's a white washed empty old tomb, but I just could never go for the happy, clappy, hands in the air, dancing around services that you folks have." At that comment, May quickly jabbed Ben in the side with her elbow. Ben jumped. "No offence to you Peter," he said sheepishly, realising who he was sitting with.

"None taken!" Peter smiled.

"Actually, it was the good Reverend himself," Ben motioned to the letter held in Peter's hand, "Father Harvey who told my great granddaddy Tommy about Christ. Tommy was a good man who brought up his family to love God and his generations followed all because of Father Harvey."

"Did your grandfather ever mention Father Harvey's accident?" Peter enquired.

"Well, I can remember my granddaddy telling me that his father, Tommy, didn't talk about it too much. He only talked about it a few times when my granddaddy asked about the old carriage in the barn.

But the story did sound a bit strange. He said that Tommy loved driving for the Father and that he was a good man, but he did in fact say that he thought that night wasn't an accident."

"How do you mean? The papers all stated that it was an accident," Peter asked, with a concerned look on his face.

"Well, that's what the folk around these parts were told by the chief of police John Barnes, and lead to believe but Tommy wasn't so sure."

"Please continue," Peter motioned.

"Apparently the story that ran in the newspaper the next day was that the police investigated the wreckage and determined that one horse had thrown a shoe and because of the reckless speed that they were travelling the horse stumbled and couldn't regain his footing, went down bringing the other horse with him. Tommy was catapulted over the front; Father Harvey was thrown out the side and killed instantly." Ben paused. "But Tommy never believed it."

"Really… Why?" Jack questioned, eager to hear the rest of the story.

"Well, when Tommy was recovering in the hospital the chief of Evensmore Police, John Barnes came to see him and Tommy told the chief that he believed that Charger, the lead horse, had been shot. But the chief would have none of it, and told Tommy that he's just had a bad accident and he was purely imagining things. But Tommy went on insisting that the horses were sound and had fresh shoes only put on two days before, but the chief wouldn't listen and told Tommy to leave it well alone. Tommy thought it all sounded very strange and asked to see the horse's remains but the chief said that they had already been disposed of due to the nature of the accident, they had to act quickly as people were extremely disturbed about the incident." Ben paused for a moment. "My granddaddy said that Tommy never trusted the police after that day and believed that it was a conspiracy and that the Father was deliberately murdered for some unknown reason. He said that he never knew why Father was in such a desperate rush to get back to Evensmore by early morning," Ben concluded.

"Well, I guess we know now," Jack said. "So did Father Daniel actually deliver the message Father Harvey was trying to stop?"

"Yes," Peter interjected, "he delivered it at the Evensmore fellowship gathering that very morning. Apparently, he did not know about the accident until after the conference had finished that afternoon, he was so devastated at the news about his best friend that he had to be hospitalised. The authorities had been determined to keep it quiet until the finish of the conference as there were so many religious officials in attendance, they did not want to cause concern or interfere with the message."

"You certainly know a lot about it," Ben stated with a grin.

"Yes, I do actually." He smiled back. "I made it a point to study the history of this area when I moved here. I also was secretly a little excited that I came to the town of the founders of the secret rapture theory."

"It's so remarkable that this is the little town from where it all started," Jack stated.

"Yes, what started in Evensmore nearly 200 years ago, has gone full circle...the truth is now revealed," Peter replied.

"WOW! I still can't believe it... I mean hidden away *all* this time," Jack said looking at everyone in amazement.

"We'll, I'm now sure that's the reason Tommy kept the carriage," Ben said. "For some reason they didn't destroy it and allowed Tommy to take it. I really don't think he honestly thought it could be restored, I think he knew that there was truth hiding somewhere there and was hoping that it would be revealed someday. He told my granddaddy that he wanted the carriage kept safely in the barn, tucked away so no one knew about it. May always chided me about that old thing taking up space, I nearly did get rid of it once, but something in me just told me to keep it there. Lucky, I guess." Ben smiled.

The others let out a small chuckle and agreed that it was very fortunate indeed.

Jophiel looked over towards the great Warrior angel standing beside the wrecked carriage, and raised his hand in salute for a job well done. The angel proudly saluted back and smiled graciously... unfurled his giant, magnificent white wings, and left his post with a blaze of glorious light for the first time in nearly two hundred years.

"You lied to me Crechus," Lothar said in a low hissing voice. "Explain yourself!"

Crechus stood before Lothar, feeling the hate emanating towards him as he quivered with fear. The hordes of other demons gathered around at a distance and waited silently to see the show slowly unravel. Teeth bared and grinning as they anticipated what was to come.

"I-I-I..." Crechus stammered, "We, well, we umm, I, and..."

"DAMN YOU!" A fist came down on the large ornate throne arm that Lothar was sitting on. "Talk, don't stammer you imbecile!" he roared.

Crechus took a deep breath trying to stifle his quavering voice and stop his fear-ridden body from shaking. He could hear chuckles coming from the other demons in the crowd. "We, we couldn't find the letter," he started, "we went all through the carriage and looked on the preacher's body for it but we couldn't find it, we then thought it may have blown out of the carriage alongside the road so I sent the scouts back to look for it. They returned with nothing, so we assumed it had been destroyed in the accident."

"ASSUMED? ASSUMED? You based this whole mission on an ASSUMPTION!" he roared, spittle flying out of his jowls, his anger growing intense. Demons stepped back further in fear; grins had turned into grimaces of trepidation, as they knew what could happen when the Master was enraged. A few left, flying out the dusty broken windows to avoid any fall out from this gathering. However, most stayed, their curiosity and taste for blood overriding any fear they felt.

Lothar continued his rage. "Do you realise how long this has taken?" he hissed venomously. "I spent years sowing this seed into those two pitiful preachers to see it finally become a common belief. The plan had worked...we had them...but you... you idiot have strengthened the enemy's mission because of this blunder. You have potentially sabotaged everything. This was to help us take as many souls as possible, to weaken them... to trick them...and now you... YOU," he pointed angrily, "careless stupid fool could have hindered this. You have potentially given Jack the evidence he needs." He quickly lunged forward and grabbed Crechus around the throat, picking him up so he was level with his evil face, his hateful gaze boring into Crechus's desperate bulging, fear ridden eyes. "I could kill you with one hand Crechus and I don't see why I shouldn't."

Crechus's eyes widened gasping from the tight grip around his throat, his arms and legs flailing trying to hold onto something to alleviate the searing pain of hanging from his neck.

"Don't send me away Master... please," he managed to wheeze out through choking breaths.

"Why shouldn't I?" he said as his grey putrid breath furled upward between them, their noses nearly touching from the closeness. Crechus started to gasp frantically, panicking as Lothar held his grip tight. He grinned as he watched his prey's life quickly ebb away.

THUMP! Lothar let go of Crechus and he fell hard into a choking and gasping heap in front of his feet.

"You *will* make amends for what you have done," he said through his clenched jaw. "Your work is not finished." He looked at the hordes of demons in front of him and all around the building and spoke, "I want you *ALL* to make Jack Daley's life a living *HELL*, go and wreak havoc on that family. He will not win this battle. Go NOW!" he screeched.

Suddenly there was a burst of thrashing panicking wings, screeches and screams as demons flew out every exit and opening in the old building to carry out Lothar's bidding.

CHAPTER TWENTY

It was early Tuesday morning when the demon of Sickness lurked near Jack Daley's house. Without any utterance the dark shadow was stealthily creeping, peering into the house windows, and moving cautiously so not to be detected by any Guardians. The demon appeared resembling every disease possible, reeking with his pungent stench, covered in cysts, yellow seeping sores and warts; parts of its greyish coloured flesh was hanging in shreds and profusely rotting. He gradually entered through the outside wall, absorbing the solid brick mass before passing through the other side. He eagerly made his way to Matthew's room, pleased that there were no Guardians and that Matthew still lay sound asleep in the early hours. Sickness dug his long silvery hooked talons into Matthew's body, tightening his grip and securing his hold on the boy.

Matthew woke with a jolt and a flood of nausea and pain rose over him like a tidal wave. His stomach lurched, cramped, and convulsed. Without having time to get to the bathroom he projectile vomited over his bed cover and started to cry out in agony.

The Guardians were first on the scene, the pungent stench hitting them in the face like a solid brick wall, they knew instantly before entering the room what was in there. They all stood watching the slimy demon work Matthew's body, slowly infecting him.

"Why weren't you here watching him?" Gabe said with annoyance looking at Matthew's Guardians. "You were supposed to protect him. Where were you, what were you doing?"

They both hung their heads and apologised at their failure in protection. "We heard a noise in the lounge room and went to investigate," one of them sheepishly replied. "It clearly was a diversion."

Seth placed his hand on the Guardian's shoulder in reassurance. "You know how the enemy works. We must be vigilant to not let our guard down," Seth said. "They obviously know about the letter and will try and attack this family; we must be alert to everything around us."

"We need reinforcements," Gabe said and they all nodded in agreement.

Jenny burst through the door upon hearing Matthew's cries. Shocked at the mess all around Matthew, she rushed over to his bedside with Jack close behind. "Oh honey," she crooned, "what's wrong?" she said with her hand on his forehead feeling his temperature rising.

"I feel sick mummy, really sick. I have sharp pains in my tummy." He wrenched forward in agony.

"Where?" Jack asked.

"Everywhere dad, it just hurts all over my tummy, and I feel so sick." With that, his body convulsed and he started vomiting again.

The demon of Sickness continued to work into Matthew's body, focusing solely on infecting him. His long silvery hooked talons had now fastened tightly to his young victims' body. *Master will be pleased*, he thought.

Jack ran out to the hallway and immediately rang the doctor.

"I'm sorry about the mess mum," Matthew said, as his eyes filled with tears.

"Don't worry about that Matthew, it doesn't matter," Jenny replied. "We've just got to get you well."

Within 10 minutes, Jack looked out the window to hear the ambulance siren coming down the road.

"They're here," he said. "Let's go!"

The small grey spirit waited until everyone was gone, its diversion had been very successful. It floated gently and quietly into Jack's office, looking around for the letter. It saw the timeworn canister and made a rapid beeline for it. It clasped the round tin in its tiny claws and then turned to leave.

"Ahem." Chale cleared his throat to draw attention.

The small spirit quickly tried to exit, but Chale lunged forward and pinned one of its wings against the wall with his sword. The tip pierced straight through the leathery membrane into the plaster.

"Eeek," it screamed in panic, flapping its free wing rapidly trying to break loose, causing its pinned wing to tear slightly from the impaling of the angelic sword.

"Drop it!" Chale said sternly.

It instantly dropped the canister with a clang and it rolled along the wooden floor.

"Why are you here?"

"M-m-master t-told me t-to steal it." It shook violently with fear looking up at the great warrior that held him captive.

"Why?"

"C-c-cause its e-evidence. It-it may ruin the plan."

"Good…Tell your master he failed." Chale smiled satisfactorily pulling out the sword from the wall and releasing his foe.

The spirit dropped to the floor.

"Leave and don't return, else I *will* finish you."

The spirit left in a flurry out the window, he got some distance before he landed looking in the direction of the old pump station. He decided not to return, he knew Lothar would execute him. He recommenced his journey but flew in the opposite direction…far away from Evensmore.

Thursday lunchtime came around very slowly and Jack was at Ben's farm for some timeout from the hospital. "How's Matthew?" Ben Jackson asked.

"He is still in hospital, they are not sure what's causing his sickness and they're still running tests," Jack replied. "Jenny is with him now."

"He's got a slime drip in his arm," Sarah said to Ben, screwing up her face in disgust at the thought.

"It's a *saline* drip sweetie," Jack said amused at his daughter's misinterpretation.

Sarah just shrugged and looked at Ben and said, "Well, it sounds yucky anyway. I'll go get Mustard ready," she said as she led Mustard over to the hitching rail.

"We've been at the hospital since Tuesday, so I thought I'd bring Sarah out for her lesson to try and get her mind off Matthew, she's been very upset and worried about him. We all have," Jack said.

"Well, doctors are pretty good these days," Ben said. "He'll be fine."

"Yeah, I hope so Ben. Listen, I'm going straight back over there as soon as we leave here. Would you mind if we left Mustard here for the night, I'll take him home tomorrow?"

"Sure, not a problem, we love having the little guy around." Ben smiled.

It was a glorious sun filled day outside, but Lora was in her darkened bedroom with several candles set out in the pattern of a five-point pentagram, along with thick heavy chalk lines drawn across the worn oak flooring. The dense black curtains were drawn and the room was dimly lit by the orange flames flickering and dancing, being pushed by a rogue breeze that had snuck under her locked door. She and Crystalyn were spending the afternoon creating incantations and rhymes. "Ah, that's a funny one!" Lora said laughing and Crystalyn giggled in response. "Hey I got one," Lora said as she started a little spell.

As they both sat on the floor in the room, Crystalyn could see the invisible blackness getting thicker and thicker; a dark cloud was drawing in on the town of Evensmore, unseen by human eyes. Crystalyn sat there and grinned at how easy it was to call them in.

Sarah and Mustard were doing a beautiful extended trot around the arena.

"Oh Sarah, he looks lovely!" May called out. "Now put him into a circle for two laps and canter down the centre line then halt."

Unbeknownst to everyone, something was watching. A dark shadow ever so slightly moved, red eyes were staring, twitching and waiting, a small goblin was hiding behind the midpoint arena post. As Mustard came cantering down the centre, the black stringy demon took his chance. He ran out in front of Mustard and leapt onto his neck, sinking his barbed teeth into the side of him. Mustard suddenly reeled sideways and groaned in agonising pain and in confusion, he panicked and bent himself back and launched upward rearing into the sky whilst letting out a deep chilling scream. The demon bit harder, also sinking his claws deeply into the pony's flesh. Mustard tilted on his hindquarters as he wrenched sideways and twisted backwards… falling to the ground landing on top of Sarah.

Work completed, the demon fled.

Mustard writhed on the ground, desperately trying to get up. He quickly scrambled to his feet and started to shake and snort as he looked down at Sarah's still, motionless body.

In a split second upon hearing the screams, Jack was by Sarah's side, crouching over her. May was already on her mobile calling an ambulance as Ben gently moved the traumatised pony away and checked him over for injury.

"No, no!" Jack cried in panic, crouched over Sarah, desperately wanting to hold her, but fearing not to touch her. All he could do was sit beside her in the dust and sob, praying aloud, "God please, please no, not my little girl. Please God save her."

"She's still breathing Jack," May stated as she stayed amazingly calm in the crisis.

They all looked up upon hearing the siren and seeing the ambulance speed into the driveway. Within minutes, she had oxygen, a neck brace and was on the stretcher in the ambulance with Jack in the back crying beside her.

THWACK! "SCREEEEECH… don't hit me, AAAAHHHH, don't hurt me," it cried as it was ducking and weaving, flapping around avoiding the angelic blade of Seth. "OOOOOOHH, please, OUCH, NO, please, please." Seth had it cornered, his blade hard pressed against the little demon's neck, a gooey green moisture started to glisten on the sword that was slowly cutting into his slimy flesh. "OOOOCH, please, I'll tell, I'll tell, Yesssss, I'll tell you everything, just don't kill me... spare me please."

"Then TELL!" Seth said sternly.

"I-I'm just following orders," he squeaked, "Master is upset that you have the letter."

"What's the plan?" Seth asked.

"I don't know," he wheezed. "We were just told to make trouble."

Seth pressed the blade harder, the slimy ooze started to flow more freely and the demon started to scream and squirm.

"I know nothing, nothing more, I swear," he cried out in pain.

"Then go and don't return." Seth stepped back and released him.

The demon whimpered and scampered away, limping and half fluttering trying to gain some lift, but his torn and tattered wings were too damaged to give flight. He limped back toward the old pump station, hurting, and complaining, however very pleased with himself at the trouble he had caused.

Jack and Jenny were at their little girl's bedside, she was asleep, but the fracture in her leg and her broken arm was causing her to writhe fitfully with pain. Jenny sat there and stroked her forehead as tears fell down her cheeks.

"What's going on Jack?" she asked, as she looked at him. "We have two children in hospital within a week? What's happening to us?"

"I don't know," he sighed in defeat. "I *just* don't know."

Lora and Crystalyn had finished playing the spell game. The candles were blown out; floor wiped clean, curtains pulled back and the orange glow of the sunset gently filtered through the open window. Crystalyn was very pleased at what they had achieved this day.

"About time you halfwits made some progress," Lothar bellowed, looking down at his horde of gaggling and salivating minions. "I want to see more of what went on today, do not let up be relentless!" He paused scanning the jostling underlings. "Where is Crystalyn?"

Slowly Crystalyn weaved through the middle of the crowd, edging gradually toward the front.

"Here sire." He bowed down low, deliberately making a show of it. The others snickered.

"Ah, Crystalyn, once I thought you were just a whiny fool, a thorn in my side, but you have proved today that you do have some worth."

"Why thank you your Majesty!" Again, he bowed low excepting the accolade, Lothar clearly enjoying his reverence.

"Continue working with the girl; create more of what you did today. She is fast becoming an asset. Better than some others you have coached in the past."

"Your wish is my command," he responded, bowing and backing away slowly into the crowd behind him, relieved that he had survived the encounter.

Chortles and jeers where heard. "Moron, crawler, sycophant," the other demons whispered and sneered, baring their teeth with hatred as he walked by.

Peter sat in his room praying for Jack and his family when his phone rang. "Peter. It's Jack!"

"Jack how is everyone?"

"Not good, Jenny fainted momentarily at the hospital and they have her in a ward there as well under observation. They think it's exhaustion but they are running tests on her too. I've had to come home and get clothes for my *whole* family. Gees Peter… what's happening, what have I done to deserve this? I thought God was here to protect my family and me. I just don't get it," Jack stated, sitting despondent in his lounge room rubbing his head in despair.

"You're under attack," Peter said. "We must pray for protection and bind the enemy, they are obviously not happy about what God has been revealing to you. That's what it's been about Jack, can't you see it now, that's why they sent those demons to torment and dissuade you all those months ago, to try and stop you from finding out and exposing the truth."

"You really think so? You really think they would go to such lengths?"

"Of course, c'mon Jack, who are you kidding here? They planted this lie nearly 200 years ago, do you think they want the truth exposed before they get any benefit from it? This is not a game, their aim is to get as many souls as possible, by *any* means or trickery. It's exactly like you said Jack. The enemy set out to deceive us all along with that falsehood and to lure Christians into that belief…it did me."

"So, you think that they are targeting my family in retaliation?"

"Yes, I do, but God is greater than Satan, so there is nothing to be afraid of, we have won, and we have the authority through Jesus Christ. We just have to apply it and speak it out. I have the rest of the church praying for your family. So, let's pray!"

"Now Lora," Crystalyn said, "it's a full moon tonight, so let's have some real fun."

"Already… we did the magic this afternoon."

"We just need to do some more… that's all," Crystalyn responded with excitement, still on a high from the praise received from Lothar.

"Sure, what do you want to do?"

"Well let's…" Crystalyn suddenly paused, and pricked an ear eastward.

"What's wrong?"

"Ah, nothing… it's nothing," and simply continued. However, Crystalyn had felt the shift, and wasn't pleased.

CHAPTER TWENTY-ONE

Jack and Peter continued to pray over the phone, asking God for protection, claiming healing, and health to his family.

Unseen by human eyes, their prayers were being answered as powerful lucent beings started plummeting earthward from the heavens into Jack's house and all around his border. The newly arrived angels formed a guard around Jack's property, strengthening and fortifying the boundary.

The hospital room where the children recovered started filling with a vivid brilliance, as the glory of the heavenly beings filled the space.

"We have the numbers now," Gabe stated.

"You can't touch me," Sickness shrieked at the angels in Matthew's hospital room, his voice full of panic and defiance. "I have a right to be here, this boy is always feigning illness."

"O really, you have no rights at all. We have every right, so leave, the prayers of God's people are more powerful than your 'so called' power," Gabe commanded.

Jack and Peter focused, unrelenting in their prayers as Peter started to claim authority over Jack's family. "I command sickness to leave in the name of Jesus, you have no authority over the Daley family, they are sons and daughters of the Most High God. Be Gone in Jesus name!"

At those very words, like a powerful electric shockwave the demon was thrown backwards off and out of Matthew's body, slamming hard against the back wall of the room with an unseen force. He lay there confused with his grey rotting wings spread and his body hunched and crumpled. The demon started whimpering and cursing as he came to, his sinuous slimy grey arms reaching out, sliding his decaying body forward again to take hold of Matthew. His silvery hooked talons clicking on the hard vinyl flooring as he slid onward towards his prey. A towering athletic angel stepped forward with his sword aflame; he swung his mighty blade, *WHACK!* The massive weapon cut cleanly through the demon's torso and a black grey sludge splashed on the hospital walls and floor. In a puff, he was vaporised, leaving just the dissipating black smoke and a sickly stench aftermath.

Over the phone Jack and Peter continued to pray together. The presence of the Lord could be sensed, like thick heavy dew it came down, blanketing them both in warmth of peace. Angelic beings all around joined them, whilst more and more angels dropped from heaven filling the house and the surrounds. The prayers from the church saints were floating upward and emanating outwards, lifting the skies and breaking through the dense foul blackness that was trying to encroach upon this family.

"PULL BACK AND RETURN!" a demon shouted back towards the heavy black mass. In a flurry and panic, they retreated and took to the skies screeching and howling in terror. Some managed to avoid the strong metallic blades of the angelic warriors descending from the heavens, others were not so lucky, leaving a trail of shadowy smoke in their aftermath.

In Sarah's room, many of the Lord's hosts had arrived. The angels felt the Holy Spirit stir within the room and an angel with the gift of healing stepped forward and lay his golden shimmering hand upon Sarah's little forehead, instantly she became well.

Jack and Peter were still talking on the home phone thanking and praising God when Jack's mobile phone rang - it was Jenny. "Hang on for a moment Peter," Jack said as he answered his mobile.

"You're not going to believe this," Jenny said.

"What's happened?" Jack said excitedly.

"Well, it's the kids… it's just crazy over here, the doctors are so confused, Matthew within minutes is back to normal. His colour returned, he's sitting up, eating like a horse, and he looks like he never was sick. The doctors can't believe it and Sarah…well," Jenny started to choke up, "it's like it never happened, her broken leg and arm are not broken anymore and all her scratches and bruises have completely disappeared. Everyone's in a frenzy of excitement here, it's…it's a miracle Jack, and the peace of God… it's like… I can't explain." Jenny started to laugh. "It's just crazy…the medical staff are just going wild with excitement.

And I'm...well, I'm great too!" she said laughing.

Jack started grinning with relief and joy. "WOW! Jen, I'm coming over right now," he said and hung up his mobile and went back to the phone. "Peter," he said, "they're healed!"

"Hallelujah." Peter raised his arms. "Thank you, Jesus, thank you," he praised dancing with joy.

In the cover of darkness, Jophiel and Chale secretly gathered in their armies. Their appearances dulled to near invisible, so the enemy could not detect them.

Jophiel addressed the many combat angels assembled before him, some stood over twelve feet tall. Their massive solid muscles bore marks of previous battles where they had vanquished countless demons. "The enemy knows about Jack finding the letter," he spoke clearly, "and they are aware of how it can obstruct their plans. Nevertheless, it is imperative that they do not find out about Jacks *other* mission. We must be extremely vigilant in keeping this from them. Do everything you can to keep them away from Jack, deter them with any means possible."

Chale spoke up, reiterating the assignment's importance, "Jacks mission will bide more time for the saints to prepare, he *must* not be found out or hindered in any way. Souls are depending on it and our King does not want any soul to perish. Therefore, be forever on Guard and prevent the enemy from finding out the real mission."

Sunday morning rolled around so quickly. The sun was brightly shining and the sky radiated the most vibrant of blues. It seemed like a thousand angels had gathered in the old church grounds, standing and watching as the saints filed into the worn church building.

Peter took his position in the front and asked his musician team to start the worship. "Let's praise God, let all of creation sing," he said to his congregation.

The angels' voices echoed out throughout the surrounds, joining in with their human counterparts, praising their mighty King and creator. With utmost worship the saints sang, their spirits lifting. Some angels were watching in awe as they could see each saint glow brightly within their hearts, physically witnessing their love for the King.

When the praise songs had finished Peter asked Jack to come forward and tell of the miracle that had occurred with his family. Many staff members from the hospital were there in church for the very first time. People started to shout and praise God when Jack had finished and in an element of spontaneity, the worship and music started. Peter decided to let his sermon go for today and just continue worshipping. Glorious songs filled the sky like rainbows of colour as both saints and angels praised their Lord God.

Jophiel stood on the rooftop of the building looking outward across his army, scanning the surrounds to ensure the enemy hadn't come to spoil this day; he suddenly became solemn remembering the fierce battle he had over a thousand years ago with Lothar. He gently rubbed his chest where the long faded calloused scar still tingled slightly when touched. *I'll be ready for you next time*, he thought. He looked over at Chale, *if it wasn't for his good friend, he would not be here.* Jophiel turned and spoke to Chale. "This is just the start you know."

"I know Jophiel... but today is the Lord's Day!" Chale smiled back unfurling his magnificent white-feathered wings, lifting his arms